MURDER ON THE SAFARI STAR

M. G. LEONARD AND SAM SEDGMAN

illustrations by
ELISA PAGANELLI

FEIWEL AND FRIENDS
NEW YORK

A FEIWEL AND FRIENDS BOOK
An imprint of Macmillan Publishing Group, LLC
120 Broadway, New York, NY 10271
mackids.com

Our books may be purchased in bulk for promotional, educational, or
business use. Please contact your local bookseller or the Macmillan Corporate
and Premium Sales Department at (800) 221-7945 ext. 5442 or by email at
MacmillanSpecialMarkets@macmillan.com.

Library of Congress Cataloging-in-Publication Data is available.

First edition, 2022
Book design by Angela Jun
Feiwel and Friends logo designed by Filomena Tuosto
Printed in the United States of America by LSC Communications,
Harrisonburg, Virginia

ISBN 978-1-250-22295-4 (hardcover)

1   3   5   7   9   10   8   6   4   2

For my Best Woman,
Claire Rakich.
With love.

M. G. Leonard

For my nephew, Sully.
Always enjoy the journey.

Sam Sedgman

Banryoku ya
Shi ha ichidan wo
Motte taru

(Translation)

Myriad green leaves
Single Bullet is
Enough for death

Ueda Gosengoku

CHAPTER ONE

CHRISTMAS IN CREWE

Pssst, Hal! Are you awake?"

Sitting up in bed, Hal blinked open his bleary eyes. His bedroom was dark, but he could smell coffee. A figure in pinstriped pajamas stood in his doorway, backlit by the landing light.

"Uncle Nat?" Hal bounced up onto his knees in delight. "You came!"

"Happy Christmas, Hal."

Hal turned on his lamp, illuminating the Christmas cards on his bedside table from Lenny, Hadley, and Mason, who were friends he'd met on his train travels. The desk at the foot of his bed was covered with loose sketches of his family, his dog, and trains—lots and lots of trains. Clustered against the wall beside a leaning tower of sketchbooks were jam jars and tins stuffed with pencils, pens, and paintbrushes. Hal loved to draw, and his favorite time to do it was on a train with Uncle Nat.

The glistening black nose of Hal's fluffy white dog, Bailey, pushed past his uncle, panting as she scrambled eagerly onto the bed, blue eyes shining, lolling tongue at the ready.

"Bailey, get off! Urgh, no!" Hal protested as she licked his face.

Uncle Nat laughed. "I thought children were up with the lark on Christmas morning."

"What time is it?"

"Six." Uncle Nat took a sip from his mug of coffee. "Bev told me to give you a prod. I think Father Christmas has been here."

Hal whooped. It had been two months since their adventure on the California Comet and, though he was trying not to get his hopes up for another train trip so soon after the last, the thought of traveling with his uncle again made lightning bolts of excitement crackle in his stomach. He raced downstairs, Uncle Nat and Bailey hot on his heels.

"Happy Christmas, pet," said his mother softly, carrying his baby sister, Ellie, in her arms, feeding her a bottle. She looked at Nat. "Will James be joining us later, for Christmas dinner?"

"I'm afraid not. He's working and then driving down to his mom and dad's."

"Oh, that's a shame."

"I'm tired. Let's all go back to bed," said Hal's dad, coming out of the kitchen.

Hal laughed. His dad's eyes were bright with mirth. He loved Christmas as much as Hal did.

"Now, Hal . . ." His dad adopted a serious tone as he followed Hal into the living room. "We've had a little chat and decided, now that you're twelve, you're too old for a stocking."

"Da-aa-ad," groaned Hal. His dad made the same joke every year.

"We took it down from the fireplace last night," his dad continued, enjoying his son's grumbling. "You'll be a teenager soon, and—"

"Then what's that over there?" Hal pointed at the stocking that he'd hung beside their gas fire the night before and which now lay, bulging, on the floor beside the tree.

"Well, I'll be!" Hal's dad scratched his head. "Where did that come from?"

"Dad!" Hal clapped his hands over his face. "Stop it!"

Uncle Nat was chuckling, perched on the arm of the sofa, as Hal's mom sank into the cushions, still cradling Ellie.

"I hope you've been a good boy this year." His dad raised his eyebrows questioningly. "If you haven't, it might be full of potatoes and coal."

"A good boy? I caught a jewel thief and solved a kidnapping! I've been a great boy!"

"Go on, pet." His mother laughed. "Open your stocking."

Hal unwrapped a yo-yo, a set of grooming tools for Bailey, a whoopee cushion (which his dad immediately blew up and pretended to accidentally sit on), a pair of pencils that doubled as drumsticks, and a deck of cards with vintage train posters on the back. Hal took his time admiring each gift and saying thank you, but as he unwrapped them, his eye kept drifting to the parcels beneath the tree, looking for a label in his uncle's sloping handwriting.

"You made fast work of that!" his mother said, as Hal dangled the stocking upside down and watched a tangerine and a walnut tumble out. She handed Ellie to Hal's father. "Let's open the tree gifts after breakfast. We're having pancakes, Nat, with bacon and maple syrup. Hal wanted a breakfast like the ones you had on the California Comet."

"But, Bev, I'm dying to see what Hal's got me for Christmas," said Uncle Nat, catching hold of her hand. "Can't we exchange our gifts first?"

"Yes, let's do that!" Hal jumped to his feet, and Bailey barked excitedly. Without waiting for his mother's reply, he dived under the tree, ignoring the prickly spines, and pulled out a rectangular parcel. "Happy Christmas, Uncle Nat." He swallowed, suddenly nervous. "I hope you like it."

Uncle Nat ripped away the wrapping paper, revealing a framed sketch of the Highland Falcon steaming across the Ribblehead Viaduct in Yorkshire. "Hal!" he gasped. "Did you draw this?"

Hal nodded.

Uncle Nat's eyes had gone glassy. He held the picture at arm's length. "It's perfect, Hal. I love it." He held his free arm out and caught Hal in a hug. "Come here. Thank you—it's the best Christmas present I could have wished for. I will hang it in my sitting room above the fireplace."

Hal blushed with pride.

"He's been working on it for weeks," his mom said, beaming.

"Well, now I feel bad," said Uncle Nat. "My present's nowhere near as good." He pulled a parcel from his pocket, wrapped in gold paper and tied with a red ribbon. "I hope you like it."

"Thank you," Hal said. The gift was the size of a large chocolate bar and felt hard. He untied the ribbon and pulled back the paper to find he was holding a tin of charcoal sticks.

"I thought you might enjoy drawing with charcoal," Uncle Nat said.

Hal felt as if all the breath had been sucked out of his lungs. He grinned wildly at the tin, trying not to show his disappointment. "Oh, wow! Uncle Nat, these are amazing! I've never drawn with charcoal before. Thank you."

Everyone in the room was staring at him, so he opened the tin to show how interested he was in the charcoal sticks. As he did, a small card fell out and tumbled to the floor. Hal picked it up.

"You'll need something to draw, of course," Uncle Nat added.

The card was hunter green, embossed with gold writing. Hal stared at it. He tried to speak, but he didn't have breath or words and found his mouth impersonating a fish's. He looked at his uncle, who was grinning like a Cheshire cat.

"We're going to South Africa, Hal," Uncle Nat said with delight. "In the February half term. We're taking the Safari Star from Pretoria all the way through Zimbabwe to see Victoria Falls, on the border of Zambia. I thought you might like the charcoal to draw the animals we'll see in the safari parks—"

But he didn't finish what he was saying because Hal was

yelling and running at him, charcoal sticks flying as he flung his arms round his uncle, knocking him off the sofa.

South Africa! Hal's heart was bursting with joy at the thought of another railway journey with his uncle. But he had no idea it would turn out to be their most dangerous adventure yet.

CHAPTER TWO

SAFARI STATION

Hal licked the edge of his thumb and smudged the lines of charcoal in his sketchbook, teasing them out to look like sharp black quills. The subject of his drawing was nibbling tree bark and glowering at him. The porcupine had a spongy nose, a salt-and-pepper Mohawk, long prickly spines, and a stubby tail. Hal leaned forward to study its face, and the spiky creature huffed, mooching off toward the train shed and flopping into a dusty hole.

"A prickly customer," Uncle Nat observed. His fair face was shaded from the glare of the sun by a broad-brimmed panama hat, and he looked every bit the European traveler in his crisp white shirt and ivory linen suit.

They were sitting at an iron table on the empty platform of Pretoria Gardens, a private rail terminal on the outskirts of the city. Before being converted to a station it had been a grand country house, and its grounds, now teeming with wildlife, had once been formal gardens. Hal thought of everyone back home in Crewe having a cold, gray February half-term holiday and grinned at the red-and-brown-speckled Nguni cattle grazing on the other side of the tracks in the morning sunshine.

***

They had landed in Johannesburg the previous night and left for Pretoria first thing that morning. It was only an hour's drive from their hotel, and Hal had been itching to explore the station. As their taxi had crawled up the white gravel drive, Hal drank in the impressive redbrick building covered with creepers and flowering vines. A bottle-green sign, half hidden in the flower beds, read ACKERMAN RAIL in peeling gold paint. A combination of excitement and hunger made Hal feel as if an army of frogs were bouncing about in his belly.

A porter took their luggage, then served them breakfast on the veranda, which was really only a wide part of the platform. The railway track was so close to the house that it looked like an eccentric driveway.

As Hal wolfed down his fruit and pastries, a man with a grin like a hungry crocodile strode toward their table. His closely cropped silver hair and beard made the suntan on his white skin more bronze, and he was dressed in a blue shirt and chalk-white trousers.

"Nathaniel Bradshaw? I'm Luther Ackerman. Welcome to Pretoria Gardens and my family's railway." He shook Uncle Nat's hand vigorously. "I'm so happy you accepted my invitation. Prepare for the experience of a lifetime! The Safari Star is a luxury hotel on wheels, the crown jewel of my fleet. We'll bring the wildlife of Africa to your window—the journey to Victoria Falls is one of the greatest in the world." His eyes darted to Hal as he finished his sales patter.

"Pleased to make your acquaintance, Mr. Ackerman," Uncle Nat replied, retrieving his hand. "This is my nephew, Harrison Beck."

"Harrison Beck?" Ackerman stepped back, studying him. Hal moved his hands behind his back in case the excitable man tried to shake them. "The railway detective I've read about in the papers?"

Hal flushed with pleasure.

"Would you like us to arrange a crime for you to solve on board?" Ackerman laughed loudly. "What would you prefer? Blackmail? Art theft? I know, how about a nice juicy *murder*?" He winked.

"I'd love to solve a murder one day," Hal said eagerly. "It's the ultimate crime for a detective."

"No, thank you," said Uncle Nat. "We've witnessed enough crime on our recent travels. We're here to see the animals."

"And the trains," Hal added. "Is it true you have a railway museum here, Mr. Ackerman?"

"Call me Luther," said the man, clapping a large hand on Hal's back and almost knocking him off his chair. "And yes!" He pointed across the track. "Over there are the engine sheds where we restore the locomotives and fit out the carriages. Beyond is the marshaling yard. Along that path is the original signal box and water tower."

He paused as an ostrich strutted past the fountain beside the veranda. "I promise you won't be disappointed." He threw his arms out wide. "Explore to your heart's content."

"Is it normal to have animals at a station in South Africa?" Hal asked.

"The animals moved in when the house was left derelict, in the 1940s," Luther explained. "They'd been living here so long when I bought it, I didn't have the heart to move them on." He looked at Uncle Nat, snapped his heels together, and bowed his head. "I've bothered you for long enough. I will be your train manager on this journey, so I'll see you on board the Safari Star."

***

"I wonder if there *will* be a crime to solve on this trip," Hal said as they crossed an iron bridge over the tracks. They were following a path through the trees to the engine sheds, and the cool shade of the foliage provided welcome respite from the heat of the sun.

"I hope not," said Uncle Nat, fanning himself with his hat. "I'd like to relax and enjoy the safari."

"But crimes are exciting to solve," said Hal, watching a beetle the size of a chestnut flying clumsily ahead of them, "and I'm good at it."

The beetle crashed into a tree trunk and tumbled to the ground.

"Be careful what you wish for." Uncle Nat laughed ruefully.

Through a gap in the trees, they could see two giant sheds straddling the tracks. A royal-blue locomotive was visible through the open doors. Hal hurried toward them, his uncle right behind him.

Inside, the sheds echoed with hammer clangs and whirring

machines. Hal and Nat climbed up to a gallery overlooking the workshop.

"*Amazing!*" Hal mouthed to his uncle as they peered down at the old carriages and locomotives in various states of repair. A scatter of sparks gushed from a trough beneath the rails, and he caught sight of a woman tinkering with the belly of a half-dismantled Class 6 loco. She wore overalls, and her pale arms were streaked with grease, reminding Hal of his friend Lenny. He leaned his sketchbook on the railing to draw her. As he smudged black lines to shade in the gleaming metal of the engine boiler, Hal saw Uncle Nat wander into view.

The mechanic came up from her trough, wiping her arms on a rag. She had short hair and a snub nose that made her look like an extremely tough pixie. She shook Uncle Nat's hand, and he pointed up to Hal.

Hal waved, then followed the gallery along to a set of stairs down to the workshop floor.

"Hal?" Uncle Nat waved him over. "This is Flo, Mr. Ackerman's sister. She's chief engineer here."

"Hi. I was just telling your uncle about Janice, the loco pulling the Safari Star." Flo had a blunt but warm manner.

"Are you the driver?" Hal asked, immediately liking her more than her brother.

"No. Sheila and Greg are the crew. I'm coming on the journey as security. You wouldn't want to be stranded on a steam train in the savanna without an engineer."

"Stranded? Is that possible?" asked Hal.

"Anything's possible." Flo shrugged. "Things here aren't shiny and new." A strange look crossed her face. "But we do a good job."

She blinked, changing the subject. "If you'd like to see the engine, come to the footplate before we leave, and I'll give you the tour."

"Thanks, I will." Hal beamed.

They said their goodbyes and, after making a lap of the workshop to look at the dismantled carriages being restored, went back outside.

"We have an hour or so before the train leaves," said Uncle Nat, as they returned along the path. "I'd like to get my hands on a newspaper."

"I want to draw the station." Hal pointed at a bench nestled among the trees. "Maybe from there."

"Lovely idea." Uncle Nat nodded. "Come and find me when you're finished."

Sitting down, Hal opened his sketchbook to a clean double page and let his charcoal skim lightly across the paper, capturing the strong horizontal lines of the platform and the vertical lines of the station. Something heavy jumped onto his lap, and he yelled at the sight of an animal the size of a small cat, with coarse sandy hair, stubby legs, and a bushy tail. It stared at him with piercing amber eyes.

"Chipo?" a boy's voice called out. "Chipo, where are you?"

The animal wheeled around, leaping off Hal as a short boy with a flattop hairstyle, brown skin, and glasses wider than his face emerged from the trees. He was wearing a faded yellow T-shirt and khaki shorts.

"There you are, Chipo!"

The animal ran up the boy's arm, coming to sit across the back of his shoulders. The boy smiled first at her, then at Hal. "She thinks you have food."

"Oh!" Hal pulled a half-eaten bag of peanuts from his pocket. "They're from the airplane."

Looking at the boy to check it was okay, Hal poured three nuts into his palm, and Chipo jumped back onto the bench, grabbing one in each paw and stuffing them in her mouth.

"You've made a friend." The boy laughed.

"What is she?" Hal stared at Chipo as she gnawed at the nuts. "A meerkat?"

"A yellow mongoose."

"She's cool." He looked up. "I'm Hal, by the way."

"I'm Winston." Chipo snatched the last nut from Hal and jumped back onto Winston's shoulders. "Where are you from?"

"England," said Hal. "I'm traveling with my uncle on the Safari Star."

"Were you drawing?" Winston nodded at Hal's sketchbook.

"Yeah, I draw trains mostly." Hal showed his sketches from the sheds. "But on this journey, I'm going to draw animals, too." He flipped to the page with the moody porcupine.

"It needs a face!" Winston laughed.

"It didn't want to sit still."

"Chipo will sit still if you give her more nuts."

As if she disagreed, Chipo leaped off Winston's shoulder and scampered away into the trees.

"Not again!" Winston said, exasperated. "Mama said I could bring her on the train if I kept her under control." He hurried after her, and Hal followed him. "Chipo, come back here! Mongooses usually live in packs, and she thinks she's the leader of ours."

Hal was pleased they were coming on the train. "Is your mom a passenger?"

"She's the safari guide." Winston peered through the bushes toward some old sidings. "She knows everything there is to know about animals in South Africa and Zimbabwe—she's a zoologist. This is the first time I've been allowed to come on the train. Normally I have to stay at home with Pa. I've promised to be helpful—run errands, stuff like that. I really want to see Victoria Falls. Mama made me bring my schoolwork with me." Winston pulled a face.

"Look, there she is." Hal pointed at Chipo, who was a few feet away beside a tree, standing on her hind legs, sniffing the air. Her ears went flat. Darting across the ground, she leaped and caught a damselfly between her paws, which she stuffed in her mouth.

Winston put his lips together and made a squeaking noise. He made to move through the bushes toward Chipo, who ran toward him, but he froze, then drew back.

"Oh no! There's Mr. Ackerman," he whispered. "Mama told me to keep Chipo out of his way." Winston grabbed the yellow mongoose and hugged her to his chest. "C'mon, let's go."

Intending to follow, Hal glanced over his shoulder. Luther

Ackerman was speaking in hushed tones to a short, sallow man in a khaki shirt and trousers. Mr. Ackerman's shoulders were hunched, his head low and secretive. Hal put his charcoal to a page in his sketchbook, as the other man nodded, passing Mr. Ackerman a roll of money held by a silver clip that glinted in the sun. Goose bumps rose all over Hal's body.

Creeping away, he knew with chilling certainty that he'd witnessed something he wasn't supposed to see. His heart was pounding. There *was* a case aboard the Safari Star, and he was going to solve it.

CHAPTER THREE

COME DIE WITH ME

Winston!" Hal ran to catch up with him. He lowered his voice. "I just saw something suspicious." He described Luther Ackerman taking the roll of money.

"It's not wrong to give someone money." Winston frowned.

"It was a lot of money, and they were hiding in the trees."

"I wouldn't say they were hiding, exactly . . ."

"Look, I drew this quick sketch." Hal showed him his sketchbook, hoping the picture would convince him. "Mr. Ackerman is being paid money."

"You're really good, to draw something so accurate so quickly." Winston nodded at the picture. "I suppose they do look suspicious," he admitted. "But so what?"

"What if they're committing a crime?"

Winston narrowed his eyes. "A crime?"

"There's something very mysterious about this." Hal leaned toward Winston, saying in a hushed voice, "I've learned to spot strange behavior, working on previous cases . . ."

"Oh! I get it." Winston hunched his shoulders and leaned in, mirroring Hal. Shooting a look over each shoulder, he put on a gravelly voice and said, "You want to play cops and robbers?"

"No." Hal straightened up. "I'm a detective."

"Yeah, me too," Winston said in his gravelly voice. "We'll both be detectives, or"—he scowled—"shall I be the bad guy? Chipo can be my henchman."

"No." Hal was getting impatient. "You don't understand. I'm a *real* detective. I've solved two cases in the last six months, a jewel theft and a kidnapping."

Winston crossed his arms. "Are you being serious?"

"Deadly," Hal said, but he could see Winston wasn't convinced.

As they walked back to the station, Hal told Winston about catching the thief on the Highland Falcon and solving the kidnapping on the California Comet. "And now I've a hunch that Mr. Ackerman is up to something," Hal said, "and I'm going to find out what it is. Do you want to help me?"

"Um . . . I don't think so." Winston shook his head. "Mr. Ackerman is Mama's boss, and she said I wasn't to annoy him, so . . ." He shrugged. "I've wanted to do this safari for ages. It's taken me months to persuade Ma to let me come. I don't want to mess it up."

"Don't you care if your mom's working for a criminal?"

"You don't know Mr. Ackerman's a criminal, and I'd rather stay out of trouble." Winston stroked Chipo's head and glanced toward the platform. "Look, I've got to go. I said I'd help the porters load the bags. See you on board the train."

Taken aback by Winston's lack of interest in having an adventure, Hal hurried across the tracks to tell his uncle about Mr. Ackerman. When he arrived on the platform, passengers were emerging from French doors, plucking canapés from silver platters held by smartly dressed attendants, chattering about the arrival of the Safari Star. Hal spotted Uncle Nat sitting at a table. He was deep in conversation with a short, ruddy man sporting a sandy mustache. The man had thinning hair combed across his head, and the deep grooves across his forehead gave the impression of a life spent thinking. As if sensing Hal's approach, both men turned their heads and his uncle smiled.

"Hal! There you are. Come and meet my old friend, Detective Erik Lovejoy. I've just discovered that he'll be joining us on the Safari Star."

"Detective?" Hal felt a jolt.

"Retired now," said Erik with a modest smile. "Thankfully."

"Did you finish your drawing of the station?" Uncle Nat asked.

Hal nodded, suddenly self-conscious in front of Erik Lovejoy, whose green eyes were bright and his stare penetrating. "You two are friends?" he asked, sitting down.

"Your uncle makes friends everywhere he goes," replied Lovejoy approvingly.

"I met Erik almost ten years ago," Uncle Nat said. "I got into a spot of bother traveling through Johannesburg. I was mistaken for someone else and thought I'd mislaid my passport, but it transpired it'd been stolen. Could have been a disaster, but Erik came to my rescue." He smiled at the detective. "And we discovered we were both rail enthusiasts."

"We were just admiring the Dolly," Erik said, nodding at a rusting locomotive in a siding across the tracks.

"That's a 19D Class," Uncle Nat said.

"Built in the 1940s." Erik wrinkled his nose as if he could smell freshly baked bread, and sighed. "A Zimbabwean model with a torpedo tender."

"Marvelous." Uncle Nat leaned back and smiled.

"Is that a British accent I hear?" A tidal wave of tweed descended into the fourth chair at their table. A woman with curly gray hair exploding from her head smiled at them all, fanning herself with both hands, her fingers squeezed by chunky gold rings. "Oh, I'm exhausted. It's so hot!"

"It is warm," Uncle Nat agreed. "I'm Nathaniel Bradshaw."

"And I'm melting!" The woman huffed out her cheeks and guffawed, making Hal smile. She waggled her eyebrows at him, delighted to get a reaction. "It's this blasted tweed. I haven't changed since I left England. Can't get into my luggage till we're aboard the train." She straightened her blouse, and Hal saw a shimmer of sweat on her pink cheeks. "Are you all going to Victoria Falls?"

"Yes, we are." Lovejoy held out his hand. "I'm Erik Lovejoy, pleased to meet you."

"Beryl Brash," she replied, draping her hand over his and fluttering her eyelashes. "The pleasure is all mine."

"Forgive my impertinence, but are you Beryl Brash the mystery novelist?" Uncle Nat asked.

"Oh, yes!" she said brightly. "Do you know my books?"

"I'm afraid I've read only one. I think it was called . . . *Come Die with Me*?"

"That's right!" Beryl Brash's eyes bulged with excitement. "A murderous dinner party where every guest is dishy, and every dish has a twist!"

"It was . . . yes, very . . . lots of plot." Uncle Nat coughed.

"Oh, *thank you*." Beryl Brash beamed.

"Are you writing a book about the Safari Star?" Hal asked.

"This is my nephew, Harrison."

"Hello, Harrison. I have indeed come on this journey hoping to be struck by divine inspiration. My readers demand one book from me a year, and I mustn't let them down."

Beryl thrust a hand to the sky. "The romance of an African sunset . . ." She snapped her head to the left. "Steaming through wild and dangerous lands . . ." Baring her teeth, she made her fingers into claws. "Surrounded by hungry lions and venomous snakes." She relaxed her hands and chuckled. "There's bound to be a tasty mystery around here somewhere."

Hal suppressed a smile, knowing he'd already found it. "Uncle Nat writes books."

"You do?" Beryl Brash swung round, ogling Uncle Nat.

"Travel books, nonfiction." Uncle Nat batted the question away with his fingers. "I specialize in train travel."

"Are *you* writing about the Safari Star?" Beryl Brash pursed her lips, unhappy about the idea of competition.

"I'll be writing a newspaper article. I have no plans to write a book."

"Good!" Beryl seemed relieved and turned awkwardly in her chair. "I wonder who else is traveling with us."

"Ours is the only train leaving today," Erik Lovejoy said. "Everyone here will be on board."

He nodded toward a couple on a double seat. They were turned toward each other, holding hands, deep in conversation, half smiles on their lips. The woman was wearing an electric-blue knotted headwrap that matched her dress and complemented her ebony complexion.

"That's Portia Ramaboa. She's a successful entrepreneur. She owns a chain of private medical clinics, bringing health care to remote areas. She's a high-profile campaigner for women's rights."

"Impressive," said Beryl Brash. "And who's her gentleman friend?" She leaned toward Erik. "Is he her lover?"

"That's Patrice Mbatha. He's a very famous soap actor, a heart-throb, and yes"—he paused dramatically—"he's her lover."

Uncle Nat cleared his throat to stop himself from laughing, as Hal studied the tall, athletic Black man. His hair was cropped short, and his pronounced cheekbones and dark eyes were sym-metrical. Hal thought about the only other film star he'd met—her face had been perfectly balanced, too.

"*My* heart is throbbing," said Beryl, clapping a hand to her chest. "Oh, he's too handsome. I can't look." She turned away. "How about those two?" She pointed her little finger at a couple strolling along the platform's edge.

"I heard Mr. Ackerman greeting them," said Erik. "Their name is Sasaki. I think they're from Japan."

The couple had stopped to watch an ostrich stalk across the tracks. Mr. Sasaki had a calm demeanor and was wearing a tailored navy jacket with dark jeans. He walked with grace and authority. Mrs. Sasaki wore a sun hat and a burgundy linen smock that hung loosely over her petite frame. She said something inaudible and rested her head on his shoulder. He put his hand to her forehead, then took her wrist and looked at his watch.

"He's a doctor," Hal said.

"How do you know that?" Beryl asked.

"He's taking her pulse."

"Nicely observed." Erik nodded, and Hal felt a glow of pride. "Hal's right. My guess would be a specialist surgeon. That's an expensive watch, designer shoes. If he's in medicine, he's at the top of his game. And look at his hands—immaculate. Surgeons take care of their hands." He winked at Hal.

"Oh, phooey! I've done doctors to death. Literally." Beryl closed her eyes. "I'll make him an acrobat, one of those contortionists who can put their feet behind their ears and fit into tiny spaces. Yes, that would be particularly handy in a mystery novel. She can be a knife thrower." She pulled a notebook and pen from her jacket pocket and scribbled something down. "I'll pretend they're on the run from the circus."

Erik Lovejoy raised an eyebrow and glanced at Hal and Uncle Nat.

A crashing sound made them all turn.

A rotund man in a gaudy striped blazer and pink shirt had strutted onto the veranda, knocking over the side table that had held the drinks of Portia Ramaboa and Patrice Mbatha.

"Watch where you're putting your tables," he barked in an American accent to a man in a waistcoat who'd immediately appeared with a dustpan and brush to clear up the mess.

Portia Ramaboa was on her feet, wiping at a dark stain on her dress. "Where are your manners?"

Patrice Mbatha jumped up, puffing out his chest. Portia put a hand on his arm as the American's slack pink eyelids drooped over his cold blue eyes.

"You want a new dress, honey? I'll buy you a new dress."

Portia didn't reply. Her mouth was open in surprise. She and Patrice clearly recognized the man.

"Amelia!" He called to a pale, thin, blond woman standing in the doorway of the old ticket office, giving instructions to a porter. He patted his leg, calling her over as one would a dog. He pointed at Portia. "Get the details of this lady's dress. I'm gonna buy her a new one." He sniffed and turned away, walking to an empty table.

"Oh-ho! I know who that is," said Beryl Brash under her breath.

"We all know who that is," Erik Lovejoy muttered.

"Mervyn Crosby," Uncle Nat said to Hal. "He's a media magnate. That's his wife, Amelia Cooper Crosby, a Texan socialite, and that must be their daughter, Nicole."

A bored-looking teenage girl was leaning on the doorframe as if she were too tired to walk. She wore a denim skirt and white T-shirt and had long blond curly hair.

"What's a media magnet?" Hal asked.

"Mag*nate*," Beryl corrected him. "Someone who owns several newspapers and television companies. Mervyn Crosby's a very powerful man."

"The way he sounds now"—Erik was glaring at Mervyn Crosby's broad back—"you'd never know he was from South Africa."

"He arrived in New York without a dime, aged eighteen, and became one of the wealthiest men in the world," Uncle Nat said. "Isn't that how the rags-to-riches story goes?"

Erik nodded, his expression stony. "He grew up in Joburg, like me. His origin story isn't so shiny."

"His television networks are tawdry," Beryl Brash said, looking

26

like she'd sucked a lemon. "They rejected a series based on my Detective Deirdre books. I was told Mervyn Crosby described them as old-fashioned nonsense." Her nostrils flared. "All that man's interested in making is reality shows about weight loss and plastic surgery. He wouldn't know a quality drama if it bit his bottom!"

Her rant was halted by the high whistle of a steam engine.

Hal's heart quickened to beat in time with the chuffing pistons, and they all turned to see the Safari Star pulling into the station.

CHAPTER FOUR

THE BIG FIVE

Coal dust peppered the air, the smell reminding Hal of his journey on the Highland Falcon. Pushing his chair back, he ran down the platform.

The locomotive was painted forest green, and the chimney, smokebox, and running board were picked out in gold, glistening in the sunlight. Above the bright red buffer beam, a nameplate screwed to the front declared the engine's name was Janice. It was the largest steam locomotive Hal had ever seen.

Including the tender, it was the length of a swimming pool, and the height of two men. He had his sketchbook and charcoal out in a second, drawing a circle within a circle, a handle in the center. On either side, like an upturned collar framing Janice's circular face, he drew the tall dark streamlining sheets.

"She's got a four-eight-four wheel configuration," he said, drawing the coupling rod that joined the wheels to the piston, as Uncle Nat came to stand beside him. "I've never seen that before."

"Janice is a South African Class 25NC. Built to haul freight through scorching desert," said Uncle Nat approvingly. "She means business."

"She's a beauty and a beast," said Erik Lovejoy, joining them. "It's an amazing restoration job. Mr. Ackerman's team are artists."

"Flo's the artist," Uncle Nat said. "Mr. Ackerman's sister. She's passionate about her locos."

"Nice of you to say so, Mr. Bradshaw." Flo leaned out from the engine cab and waved down at them. "Want to climb up and have that tour of the footplate I promised you?"

Hal snapped his sketchbook shut and bounded over to the ladder, followed by his uncle and Erik. They didn't need to be asked twice.

Climbing up, Hal scrambled onto the footplate and grinned at Flo. "Thanks."

"This is Sheila and Greg," Flo shouted over the hiss of the boiler.

Sheila was a wiry woman with russet-brown skin and short hair. She wore a green polo shirt and slacks and was standing at the controls. Hal guessed she was the driver. Greg was a stocky man with leathery olive skin. He wore the same uniform as Sheila and a grubby cap.

Flo grinned. "Best driving team this side of the Limpopo River. Eh!" She smacked the back of Erik's hand as he reached out to touch the regulator. "Look with your eyes, not your hands. You could burn yourself."

"Of course. Sorry." Erik looked down, embarrassed at being told off.

Hal felt a pang of warmth for the man who'd exhibited no more self-control than a curious boy.

"I've never been on the footplate of a more impressive loco," Erik mumbled.

"You must have to shovel a lot of coal," Hal said to Greg.

Greg shook his head. "Janice uses a stoker: a giant screw below our feet. As it turns, it collects the coal in the tender and delivers it right into the heart of the firebox."

"Made in Glasgow, wasn't she?" Uncle Nat said as he admired the cabin.

Flo nodded.

"In Scotland?" Hal was surprised.

"The North British Locomotive Company sold engines all over the world," Uncle Nat said. "Janice would have come to Africa on a ship."

"It must have been a very big boat," Hal said. "She's really heavy."

Uncle Nat nodded. "Some of the ships sank. There are drowned steam trains lying on the ocean floor to this day."

"Well, there'll be no drowning on our journey," said Flo. "There are barely enough water stops to fill Janice's tender. Steam's dying out in South Africa."

"I traveled on an A4 Pacific that filled up from water troughs under the track," said Hal.

"Water is precious in the savanna," said Flo. "That's why Janice has a huge tender."

"Over eleven thousand gallons of water and nineteen tons of coal," Erik marveled. He looked at Hal. "More than twice as much as an A4."

"I can't think of anything finer than driving a loco and seeing elephants and rhinos from the footplate," Uncle Nat said to Sheila.

"I see elephants and lions," Sheila replied, "but never a rhino. They've been hunted almost to extinction. Although there's always Rhino Rock."

"Rhino Rock?" Hal asked.

"A rock formation that, from the south, looks like a male rhino with a horn. It's so convincing that it's scarred by bullets from hunters. When we pass it, passengers think they're seeing the real thing and take photos."

"Surely no one would mistake a rock for a rhino?" Erik laughed.

"You can judge for yourselves tomorrow evening when we're going round the Hook—a huge curved bit of track just after Mooketsi," Greg replied. "You can't miss it."

"Don't you tell people it's a rock?" Hal asked.

"No," Flo replied. "They are so happy when they think they've seen a real rhino in the wild. Why disappoint them?"

***

Hal and Uncle Nat were collected from the footplate by a smiling attendant with braided hair, also wearing the green uniform. She led them down the platform to their carriage. "Here you are, gentlemen." Opening a door halfway along the nine-carriage train, she gestured them inside with a white-gloved hand. "Your luggage is in your compartment."

Hal darted up the steps, eager to see inside the train. The carriage was lined with cherry-red wood paneling, scarred by dents and scratches from trolleys and suitcases, and there were threadbare patches on the forest-green corridor carpet.

"You are sharing the carriage with Ms. Brash," she said, showing them to a door. "This is your deluxe suite."

"A deluxe suite?" Uncle Nat frowned. "I was expecting a standard compartment."

"Mr. Ackerman wishes you to have the best experience of the Safari Star." She handed him a brass key with a leather fob. "My name is Khaya." She pronounced it *KAH-yah*. "If you need anything, pull the bell cord. It will be my pleasure to assist you. We have only a small number of guests on this journey—peak season isn't until May." She bowed and stepped back. "In one hour, Mr. Ackerman will be welcoming all the Safari Star's passengers in the observation car, at the rear of the train. He asks kindly that you arrive in good time."

"Thank you, we will," Uncle Nat said.

Khaya gave a short bow and left.

"A deluxe suite!" Uncle Nat looked at Hal. "It must be big."

Hal unlocked the door, sliding it open. "Oh, wow!" He stepped inside, turning left, then right. In front of him was a small table with a silver platter of sandwiches and fruit. On either side of it were armchairs. Above it hung a flat-screen TV, and to the left a two-seater sofa marked out a lounge area. Opposite that were a built-in wardrobe and drawers. "We've got real beds!" Hal exclaimed, flopping face-first on the one beside the window.

Rolling over, he called to his uncle, who'd opened the door at the far end of the compartment. "Can I have this one?"

"You may have whichever bed you like."

"What are you looking at?" Hal bounded to his side and looked under his uncle's arm. "We've got our own bathroom? With a *bath*! Oh, this place is fancy." He thought about how wonderful having a bath would be, with the water sloshing about as the train rattled down the tracks.

"What's through there?" He pointed to a door at the other end of the compartment.

"I think it's a connecting door. It must lead into Beryl's room. It's probably locked." Uncle Nat went to the drawers with his bag, transferring some books and his journal inside. "The Safari Star was once one of the most glamorous trains in the world. It was the height of luxury, but it's looking a little tired now. I can see why Mr. Ackerman is keen for me to write about it. He needs more paying customers."

Hal sat down at the table, picking up a tiny triangle of cucumber sandwich and jamming it into his mouth. "Uncle Nat"—he swallowed—"I need to talk to you about something."

"Is everything okay?" Uncle Nat looked at him over his glasses.

"I'm not sure." Hal pulled out his sketchbook and put it on the table. "I saw Mr. Ackerman doing something odd." He pointed to his drawing. "He took a roll of money—a lot of money—from this man. They were hiding in the trees. It looked like they didn't want to be seen. Like their activity was . . ." He paused. "Criminal."

Uncle Nat came over and looked down at the sketch. "How odd."

"Do you think we should tell Erik Lovejoy?"

"Goodness! No. Hal, he just retired. He's on this train for a well-earned rest." Uncle Nat chuckled. "The train hasn't even left the station and you're hunting for a crime to solve." He gestured at Hal's drawing. "This could be perfectly innocent."

"Or it could be a bribe. He could be blackmailing someone, or selling something illegal, or . . ."

"Stop!" Uncle Nat was laughing now. "You're quite right. It could be any of those things. In fact, that suspicious gentleman could be paying Luther Ackerman to bake a giant cake for his mother's secret birthday party!"

Hal frowned at Uncle Nat's joke.

"The thing is, Hal, we don't know what they were doing. Let's not jump to conclusions."

"I'm not accusing anybody of anything," Hal replied defensively, "not until I've got proof, anyway, but I know I saw something I shouldn't have." He looked down at his picture. "Mr. Ackerman is up to something."

"He may very well be, but he is also the owner of this train and the person who gave us this compartment to stay in." He opened a drawer. "Oh, look." He lifted out a pair of binoculars. "You can use these to spot the Big Five."

Hal took the binoculars, aware that Uncle Nat was changing the subject. "I keep hearing people talking about the Big Five. What are they?"

"The animals everyone hopes to see on safari." Uncle Nat counted them off on his fingers. "The lion, the leopard, the Cape buffalo, the African elephant, and the rhinoceros."

"But why those five? There are lots of animals in South Africa—I've seen more than five already."

"Back when safaris were about hunting, those were the hardest animals to hunt." He opened the wardrobe and his suitcase. "There's a book on the table."

Hal picked it up. "'*Animals of South Africa*,'" he read out loud, and flipped through the pages. "Hey, it's Chipo! It says here, mongooses are related to meerkats." He paused. "Oh yuck! She eats lizards and spiders!"

"Who's Chipo?"

"A yellow mongoose I met. She belongs to Winston, the son of the safari guide on the train." He looked at his uncle. "It was

Chipo who led me to the clearing where I saw Mr. Ackerman."

Uncle Nat sighed. "Be careful, Hal. Luther Ackerman knows you're a skilled detective. If he *is* up to something, he'll be watching you. I think you'd be better off letting this go. Why don't we just enjoy the safari, eh?"

Hal nodded, looking down at the picture of the yellow mongoose. Now even Uncle Nat was turning his back on adventure. Why was everybody so concerned about upsetting Mr. Ackerman? Hal wasn't scared—if he *was* doing something illegal, then Hal was going to catch him. "Sherlock da Vinci is on the case," he muttered to himself.

"What?"

"Just . . ." Hal smiled brightly. "We don't want to be late."

CHAPTER FIVE

ACKERMAN'S ADDRESS

On their way to the observation car, Hal heard raised voices. A man and a woman were arguing in one of the sleeping compartments.

"*I cannot believe what you're asking of me!*" the man shouted.

"I'm asking you to be civil." Hal recognized Portia Ramaboa's commanding voice. He paused to listen. "Don't make this trip about him."

"After what he did to me? You expect me to sit and smile while he charges up and down like a silverback gorilla. If I'd known he'd be on this train—"

"That is *exactly* what I expect you to do." Portia cut him off. "You're an actor, aren't you? So *act*. There is more than your pride at stake here." Her voice softened. "Please. For me."

"Hal, are you coming?" Uncle Nat had reached the end of the corridor and was looking back at him. He hurried forward, not wanting to be caught eavesdropping.

The observation car was bright and airy, with high windows.

It was furnished with brocade armchairs, their backs to the wall. Beryl Brash was reclining on a comfy armchair near the glass doors at the end of the carriage; they opened onto a balcony over the tracks. Through the doors Hal could see Luther Ackerman

standing beside a tall woman in dark green combat trousers, with a hunting rifle slung over her back, its leather strap on her shoulder. Hal guessed she was Winston's mom. He spotted Winston sitting hunkered down in the corner behind Beryl and waved.

On the sofa beside Beryl's, Mervyn Crosby was absentmindedly picking his nose. His wife and daughter were looking bored. Erik beckoned Hal and Uncle Nat to a sofa across from him. Mr. and Mrs. Sasaki nodded politely in greeting as they sat down, introducing themselves as Ryo and Satsuki. Hal resisted the temptation to ask Ryo Sasaki if he was a surgeon.

"Ah, Mr. Mbatha and Ms. Ramaboa, welcome. Take a seat." Luther Ackerman made a grand gesture as Portia and Patrice entered the room. Patrice was moving stiffly, suppressing his anger, but Portia was poised and serene.

"Now that we're all here, I shall begin." Mr. Ackerman stepped into the room from the balcony, framed by the double doors, making the marshaling yard his backdrop.

"This can't be all the guests, can it?" Hal whispered to his uncle. "There are so many empty seats!"

Before Uncle Nat could reply, Luther Ackerman clapped his hands together. "Welcome aboard the Safari Star, Ackerman Rail's finest luxury train! I am your train manager, here to ensure your journey is unforgettable. We are so happy you chose to travel with us, and look forward to sharing the wild treasures of South Africa and Zimbabwe with you.

"Today, we journey east, through the plains of Mpumalanga, then on through the lower peaks of the Drakensberg mountains. Overnight we will venture north to the station at Hoedspruit beside the world famous Kruger National Park, in time for tomorrow's safari. The park stretches over five million acres of land, which bristle with hundreds of species of mammals and birds—including Africa's Big Five, so bring your binoculars."

There was an appreciative murmur from the train guests.

"We will return to the train in the afternoon for high tea, before heading north once more toward Beitbridge. When you wake up on our second morning, we'll be at the border between South Africa and Zimbabwe. After breakfast and the requisite paperwork checks, we will steam onward through Zimbabwe's beautiful vistas until we are deep in the Hwange National Park, ready for an afternoon safari. Our journey reaches its dramatic conclusion the next morning, when we will cross the breathtaking Victoria Falls Bridge, reaching our final destination in Zambia.

"You will witness nature's greatest wonders from the comfort of your five-star luxury suites. There will be many opportunities to experience the wildlife from closer quarters, and you will be guided at all times by our experienced and knowledgeable zoologist, Liana Tsotsobe."

Winston's mother stepped forward. "Thank you, Mr. Ackerman." She smiled. "It is my pleasure and responsibility to lead two safari expeditions on this journey. You will be seeing a rich variety of wildlife on this trip. It may seem obvious, but these are *wild* animals. When outside the train, in the parks, you must always follow my instructions. Nature is beautiful, but she is dangerous, and even on land fenced in by man we must be respectful and cautious at all times."

"Is that why you're carrying a gun?" asked Beryl, ogling the weapon.

"My rifle is only ever used as a last resort." Liana's hand went to the gun's leather strap. "It is for your protection. Unfortunately, a tranquilizer gun will not bring down a charging animal fast enough to save your life."

"I see!" Beryl's eyes were wide.

"I'll keep you safe." Mervyn Crosby leaned over his wife and patted Beryl's knee. "I'm a sharpshooter." He looked up at Liana with a crooked grin. "Nothing gets the blood singing like the thrill of the hunt—am I right?"

"While you are traveling on Ackerman's railway, no one is permitted to carry or use a gun but me," said Liana with authority.

"Oh, please," Mervyn Crosby scoffed. "I'm a damn fine hunter. Moose, elk, bear, raccoon . . ." He thumped his chest proudly. "I've shot 'em all."

"Let's get back to the itinerary," Mr. Ackerman insisted, glancing nervously at Liana, who was glaring at Mr. Crosby.

"Hey now, listen," Mr. Crosby said, ignoring him. "I've been shooting big game in Africa for years. Takes more than a couple of lions to scare me. I've got the heads of four of the Big Five mounted on my wall back home—all I'm missing is a rhino. It would be nice to complete the set. That's why I brought my hunting rifle, and that's why I'm on this train."

Everybody in the carriage looked at Mervyn Crosby in shocked silence. It was Patrice who finally spoke, through gritted teeth. "The rhinoceros is one of the most endangered species on the planet." Portia put her hand on his arm.

"Can't be harder to kill than an elephant," said Crosby, mistaking his incredulity for respect. "You want to see the size of the one I bagged? I've got a picture, look." He pulled his phone from his blazer pocket.

"*Stop it*, Pop!" Nicole Crosby had her head in her hands. "Nobody wants to see."

"When I use a gun, Mr. Crosby," Liana said, "it is to save lives, not take one. This is not a hunting expedition. This is a rail safari.

You will not be shooting any animals on our journey. Not only will I not allow it, it is prohibited by law."

"What if I pay?" Mervyn Crosby said, ignoring her and addressing Luther Ackerman. "I'll double my ticket price, all of our ticket prices"—he gestured to his family—"if you let me hunt from the train. If I bag a rhino, I'll pay extra for you to strap the corpse to the roof so I can ship it home."

"I'm afraid that won't be possible," said Mr. Ackerman, flashing a placatory smile. "It is illegal, for one thing, and—"

"Who's gonna know? C'mon, everyone's got their price." Crosby pulled out his wallet. "What if I pay triple? Quadruple?"

Mr. Ackerman hesitated. "I . . . Mr. Crosby." He smiled again and pressed his hands together. "I think we have strayed from our topic. Let's discuss this privately—why don't you come to my office later? It's the train manager's compartment on the other side of the lounge. I can explain our hunting policy to you in more detail, and I'm afraid I will have to ask you to bring your gun. We'll . . . look after it for you, just for the duration of the trip."

He clapped his hands together to signify the topic was closed and smiled at them all. "Liana is a fount of knowledge when it comes to the wildlife of South Africa and Zimbabwe. She's here to answer any questions you may have during our journey together."

Liana was staring stonily at Mervyn Crosby, who was either unconcerned or unaware.

"Now, I think it's time for a toast"—Mr. Ackerman lifted a bottle of champagne from a bucket of ice in a stand beside Beryl— "to celebrate our great railway adventure."

Khaya stepped forward with a tray of empty glasses. Mr.

Ackerman popped the champagne cork, and everybody politely applauded as he filled the glasses.

People started talking, introducing themselves to one another as the glasses were passed around, although no one spoke to Mervyn Crosby. Winston appeared next to Hal's seat.

"Uncle Nat." Hal tugged his uncle's sleeve. "This is Winston and Chipo."

Chipo leaped up onto the arm of the sofa.

"Pleased to meet you." Uncle Nat smiled at Winston, then turned his attention to Chipo. "You really do have a yellow mongoose. How wonderful. Is she tame?"

"She's Chipo." Winston chuckled. "She does what she wants. I try to train her, but . . ." He shrugged.

"Excuse me, Nat, but have you met Portia Ramaboa?" Erik asked, and Uncle Nat stood up to introduce himself.

Winston sat down on the sofa beside Hal. He glanced at Mr. Ackerman, who was laughing and sipping champagne with Beryl. Lowering his voice, he said, "There's something I think I should tell you."

"About Mr. Ackerman?" Hal whispered.

"Let's not talk here," Winston said. "Follow me." He lifted Chipo onto his shoulder.

The train lurched forward, and the engine whistle sang out. Hal grinned. The adventure had begun.

CHAPTER SIX

SPIDER BITES

Slipping out of the observation car, Hal followed Winston down the train, Chipo running before them.

"Where are we going?"

"You'll see."

"Did you hear that awful Mr. Crosby say he wants to shoot a rhino?"

Winston nodded. "He's a trophy hunter."

"What's that?"

"A person who pays money to hunt animals but doesn't do any hunting. Someone drives them close to an animal, they shoot it and take home its skin or its head, boasting about how brave they are." He grimaced. "I hate it."

"Why would anyone want to do that?"

Winston shrugged. "Makes them feel strong and powerful, I guess. But it's not *real* tracking and hunting. I'd like to take Mr. Crosby's guns away and leave him stranded near a pride of lions." He chuckled. "Then we'd know how brave he is."

They reached the lounge car, in the middle of the train. It had wide windows and an olive carpet threaded with gold. Two whirling ceiling fans hung from an ivory-painted ceiling. An upright piano stood against one wall, opposite a long bar, with shelves of liquor bottles gently chiming as the train moved.

Chipo jumped up to run along the bar, then onto Winston's shoulder.

"There aren't many passengers on this safari," Hal said, taking in the number of leather chairs. "The train could fit way more."

"It used to be packed in peak season, but Mama says Ackerman's railway has fallen on hard times." They passed a chaise longue with a popped seam and stuffing escaping. "And rich people want everything to be perfect."

"I think the Safari Star is perfect," Hal said, noticing a low bookcase crammed with board games, tatty paperbacks, and travel books. One of Uncle Nat's books was on the shelf, and he smiled.

"Mama's worried she might lose her job if things get worse. But I'm glad there are so few passengers today, because I wouldn't be able to come if the train was full."

"I think Mr. Ackerman gave my uncle our tickets so that he'd write about the Safari Star in the newspaper," said Hal. "Maybe more people will come after they've read about it."

"Depends what he says."

Hal fell silent as they left the lounge. He wasn't sure what Uncle Nat thought of the train.

"If lots of people wanted to book tickets, Mr. Ackerman could turn away people like Mervyn Crosby."

"He won't really be allowed to shoot a rhino, will he?" Hal asked.

Winston shook his head. "He'll be lucky to even see one. There's hardly any left."

"Aren't rhinos protected?"

"They are, mostly, but it's complicated. Some reserves have special licenses to breed rhino to be hunted, and they make big money from it. It's helped save the species. The worst people are the poachers. They break into game reserves and kill rhinos for their horns."

"Their horns?"

"A rhino's horn is worth more than its weight in gold. Poachers kill the rhino and saw off its horn, to sell." He shook his head.

Hal was taken aback. "Why is the horn so valuable?"

"Because it's rare. Rich people make jewelry out of it and wear it, so everyone knows they have money." Winston shrugged. "Other people think rhino horn has healing powers. They grind it into powder and take it like medicine."

"Does it work?"

"Mama says they might as well eat sand." Winston shook his head and sighed. "And then there are the humans who are bad right through the middle, who enjoy killing." He looked at Hal over his glasses. "I think Mr. Crosby is a rotten one."

Hal nodded. "He's rude."

"And uglier than a baboon's bottom."

Hal laughed.

"This is my compartment," Hal said as they passed the door.

"Nice—a deluxe suite." But Winston didn't slow his stride, and Hal wondered where they were going.

They passed through the dining car and then a service car—a cacophony of clattering kitchen percussion over the rhythm of wheels on rails. The carriage beyond was old and hadn't been refurbished as recently as the guest carriages. The paintwork was scratched, and tatty linoleum lay on the floor instead of carpet. Winston slid open a compartment door, and Chipo darted in.

"This is mine and Mama's room."

The compartment had two bunks bolted to one wall and was hot inside. Winston grabbed the lip of the window and slid it down into the body of the train to let in a breeze. Hal caught the thick scent of summer trees and smiled.

Chipo sprang down onto the bottom bunk, and Hal perched beside her. "So . . ." He looked conspiratorially at Winston. "Why are we here?"

"Chipo's hungry," Winston replied, sitting cross-legged on the floor and taking a clear plastic box from the front pocket of a rucksack on the floor. "You're not scared of spiders, are you?" He peeled back the lid. "Don't worry, they're dead." He plucked out a dark bundle of curled-up legs. "Hey, Chipo, look—yummy spider."

Mesmerized, Hal watched the mongoose grab the spider from Winston's fingers and stuff it into her mouth. "Where did you get them from?"

"What do you think I was doing in the trees when I met you?" Winston grinned. "I got some juicy ones, too." He pulled a bigger spider from the box, and Hal shrank back.

"You said you'd discovered something about Ackerman?" Hal pressed, as passing trees threw dappled shade into the compartment.

"I have," Winston said, his eyes alight. "After I helped the porters with the bags, they told me to give the message to Mr. Ackerman that we were ready to go. And when I was outside his office door, I heard him talking on the phone."

"What did you hear?"

"He said . . ." Winston closed his eyes, uttering each word slowly as he replayed the conversation in his head. "'I understand the severe risks, Mr. Leon. The plan is in place and special arrangements have been made. Your client will not be disappointed. I give you my word.'"

"Who's Mr. Leon?" Hal wondered out loud, immediately picturing the man he'd seen handing Mr. Ackerman the money.

"Not a clue," said Winston brightly. "You're the detective—I thought you'd figure it out."

Hal chewed his lip. "It sounds like Mr. Ackerman's being paid by Mr. Leon to do something illegal. I wonder what it is . . ."

Winston fed Chipo another spider.

"Can I draw her while you're feeding her? Drawing helps me think."

"Sure," Winston replied. "Eating is the only time she sits still."

Hal took out his sketchbook and tin of charcoal. As he sketched the heart shape of Chipo's head, he thought about the telephone call. Luther Ackerman was obviously working for the mysterious Mr. Leon, but what "special arrangements" had been made? What was "the plan"? He drew the little blunt triangles of Chipo's pinned-back ears and the ring of shadow around her amber eyes. "Do a lot of people have pet mongooses?"

"No. Chipo's been with me since I was little. Her colony was attacked by an eagle. Chipo's mama tried to protect her pups, but the eagle carried her away. Mama found Chipo crying and brought her home. The other pups didn't make it. I helped wean her, and when we tried to release her back into the wild, she didn't want to go." He rubbed his finger under her chin. "She'd decided me and Mama were her colony."

51

"Did your mom teach you to wean her?"

Winston nodded. "I grew up on my grandparents' nature reserve. We took care of lots of different animals."

"You don't live there anymore?"

"We had to sell the reserve when my grandparents passed away. We live in an apartment in Pretoria now. Mama's a vet, part-time, and a safari guide, and Pa's a plumber, but we're saving up. One day, we're going to buy the reserve back and fill it with animals. I want to be a vet, like Ma." He fed Chipo another spider. "I like animals a lot more than people."

"I can see why." Hal smudged the blob he'd drawn for Chipo's nose with his pinkie and thought of his dog, Bailey.

The compartment door opened, and Liana Tsotsobe smiled at them. "I see you've already made a friend, Winston."

"Mama." Winston got up. "This is Hal."

"I just met your uncle, Hal. We suspected you three might be together." Hal stared as Liana lifted the hunting rifle from her shoulder by its leather strap. "Don't worry, it's not loaded. I wear the rifle when I meet the guests to make a point about how dangerous the wild is." She squatted down, pulling a wooden box out from under the bunk. "Usually it has the effect of making people do as I say, but not today." She opened the lid and placed the gun inside, next to a cardboard box of bullets. "There, it's gone now." She closed the case and smiled at the boys. "You're drawing?"

Hal turned the pad round.

"Chipo! That's very good."

"Let me see." Winston leaned over. "Look, Chipo, it's you." The mongoose lifted her head and sniffed the air.

"I can't wait to go on safari," said Hal, closing the sketchbook. "I'm going to draw every animal I see."

"You'll see plenty," Liana said. "If you do as I say, we can get quite close."

"Mama, do you know someone called Mr. Leon?" Winston asked.

"I don't think so." Liana frowned. "Why?"

"No reason," Hal said, getting to his feet. "If everyone's left the observation car, I should probably go." He looked at Winston. "Will I see you at dinner?"

"We'll be eating back here with the crew in the service cars," said Liana. "But we'll see you early tomorrow morning, for safari." She looked at Winston. "And you'd better make a start on that schoolwork, *nunu*, if you want to come along."

"Yes, Mama." Winston rolled his eyes as he opened the door for Hal.

"I'll let you know if I discover anything," Hal whispered, and Winston nodded.

As Hal walked back to his compartment, he was buzzing at the familiar thrill of having a case to solve. What was Mr. Ackerman up to? Who was Mr. Leon? And what was their secret plan? A thought struck him. Mr. Ackerman had asked Mr. Crosby to come to his office after the introductory drinks. That conversation must be taking place right now. Hal hurried past his compartment, remembering that a door with a thin metal plaque that read TRAIN MANAGER was in the next carriage. As he approached it, the door opened. He shrank back as Mervyn Crosby stepped out.

"Knew I could count on you, Luther." Mr. Crosby was shaking Mr. Ackerman's hand. "Oh, and about my gun . . ."

"You can keep hold of it, of course." Ackerman gave him a conspiratorial smile. "I had to say that in front of the other guests, you understand?"

Mr. Crosby laughed. "I do."

Hal shuddered. He had a horrible suspicion he knew who Mr. Leon was and what the secret plan might be, and he didn't like it one bit.

CHAPTER SEVEN

DINNER WITH ANIMALS

Uncle Nat was dressed for dinner, sitting at the table in their compartment, writing in his journal. "I'm just doing a spot of work," he said as Hal came in. "Did you have fun with Winston?"

"We fed Chipo dead spiders."

"Marvelous," Uncle Nat said, without looking up.

Hal wanted to talk to his uncle about the exchange he'd witnessed between Mr. Ackerman and Mr. Crosby, but he didn't want to interrupt. Instead, he opened his suitcase, taking out the pair of navy chinos and a white polo shirt that he'd brought to wear at dinner, and got changed.

"Ah, good, you're ready," Uncle Nat said, lifting his head as Hal looked at himself in the mirror. "Very smart."

"Uncle Nat, can I talk to you about something?"

"Of course." He returned the pen to his top pocket. "But let's do it over dinner—I'm starving."

When they arrived in the dining car, it was empty, except for

Erik Lovejoy, who was alone at a table for two. A waiter greeted them and took them to a table for four, set with crystal glasses and silver cutlery on a pristine white tablecloth.

"I can see you're itching to tell me something," Uncle Nat said as they sat down beside each other. "What is it? I'm curious." He tore a corner of bread from the roll on his side plate and popped it in his mouth.

"Well . . ."

Hal was about to tell his uncle about the exchange he'd overheard when the two men concerned, Luther Ackerman and Mervyn Crosby, strode into the dining car, followed by Mrs. Crosby and Nicole. Mr. Ackerman brought them right over and sat them at the next table, drawing back the chair for Amelia.

"I'll tell you later," he said under his breath.

Uncle Nat glanced at the Crosbys and nodded.

Portia Ramaboa and Patrice Mbatha were shown to a corner table, looking composed, but once they'd sat down, they began whispering furiously to each other. Hal guessed they were still arguing about the man Patrice hated, and he thought he knew who that man might be.

Beryl strode in with a checkered pashmina thrown over her shoulders and brazenly sat herself down opposite Erik. "They've sat us together!" she purred. "I suppose they think we're both"— she leaned forward and enunciated the word—"*unattached.*"

Erik turned bright red, and Hal had to look away to stop himself from laughing.

The waiter brought Ryo and Satsuki Sasaki over to join their table. Uncle Nat stood up, and so did Hal.

"Good evening," Ryo said. "May we join you?"

Satsuki bowed her head, and Hal copied her.

"Of course," Uncle Nat replied, and they all sat down. "Tell me, Mr. Sasaki, are you a doctor?"

"I'm a surgeon—and please, call me Ryo."

"How about that." Uncle Nat beamed at Hal. "Hal guessed you were in medicine."

"I saw you taking Mrs. Sasaki's pulse," Hal admitted. "I hope you're not unwell?"

Satsuki looked confused, and Ryo Sasaki translated the word *unwell*. She shook her head, putting her hands on her tummy. "A baby is coming."

Hal and Nat congratulated them as a white plate with a tiny salad of three leaves, two walnuts, a slice of pear, and a drizzle of sauce was placed before each of them.

"Satsuki works at a Shinto shrine, in Kyoto," Ryo said, giving her an encouraging smile.

"What's a Shinto shrine?" Hal asked.

"Shinto is . . . ah . . ." Satsuki chuckled to herself as she searched for the right word. "Like religion, but also a way of life. Shrines are"—she interlocked her fingers—"connecting with nature, with ancestors, with the past."

"There are Shinto shrines all over Japan," said Ryo. "They are peaceful places. Many people visit them, no matter their religion."

Mervyn Crosby bellowed out a loud laugh at the next table, and Satsuki's face darkened. She shook her head.

"In Shinto, all spirits in nature are gods. *Shinto* means 'the way of the gods,' 'the way of nature.'" She took a sip of water. "Some bad people have no respect for nature at all."

"We've always wanted to go on safari together," said Ryo, taking his wife's hand. "But Satsuki's not happy to find Mr. Crosby here. He is behind a project to build a super casino on an ancient forest site near Kyoto. This would be a disaster for our home. Satsuki helped to organize the protests."

"Good for you," Hal said feelingly, and Satsuki smiled.

"I haven't been to Japan in years," said Uncle Nat wistfully. "The Shinkansen are one of my favorite trains, exquisite machines."

"Bullet trains?" Hal asked.

"Yes. The nickname 'bullet train' comes from the shape of their noses and their speed. They can travel up to two hundred miles per hour."

As the appetizers were eaten, collected and replaced with a main course, the Sasakis and Uncle Nat spoke about Japan.

"That's more like it," Mr. Crosby roared approvingly as a steak was put in front of him. "Meat so rare it's still got a heartbeat."

"Would you mind keeping your voice down?" Erik said politely, turning round in his chair. "We're trying to have a conversation."

Beryl was so delighted by Erik telling Mervyn Crosby off that she made a wailing giggling noise, and suddenly everyone in the dining car was staring at him.

"What are you all looking at?" Mervyn Crosby growled. "Haven't you ever seen a man get excited about eating a decent bit of beef before?"

No one replied.

"You wait till I've got myself a nice bit of juicy rhino steak," he goaded them. "Then you'll really hear me make a noise."

Patrice jumped to his feet, his chair scraping backward. Portia grabbed him and yanked him back down again.

"Pop, *stop*." Nicole sank down in her chair, her shoulders up by her ears. "You're so embarrassing!"

Amelia Crosby was sitting in silence beside her daughter, looking pained and not eating.

"You wouldn't really eat a rhino, would you?" Hal hadn't meant to say the words out loud, but Mervyn Crosby was already turning his head to look at him.

"You think they're cute, do you, kid? Let me tell you, rhinos are killers. That horn is for fighting, for gouging and stabbing. They'd rip the meat off your bones and eat you for dinner without a thought." He carved off a chunk of steak and chewed it with his mouth open. "We eat meat, like they do. We kill it first, just like they do. It's nature."

"Rhinos are herbivores! And cows aren't endangered," said Hal, trying not to get upset. "Neither are chickens, or sheep. You don't want to kill a rhino because you're hungry. You want to kill a rhino for *fun*!"

"Damn right I do. Hunting *is* fun. The Japanese"—he pointed at the Sasakis—"they hunt whales. You Brits"—he nodded at Hal—"you hunt foxes and pheasants. Man's hunted since the dawn of time."

"*If you want to kill one of the last rhinos on earth for fun*"—Hal was on his feet—"*YOU'RE EVIL!*"

"Hal," Uncle Nat said quietly, putting a hand on his arm, "don't listen to him. No one is going to shoot a rhino. Sit down."

"Gentlemen, gentlemen!" Luther Ackerman hurried toward them. "Is this the kind of conversation you want to have over dinner? I think not, hmm?" His eyes flicked nervously around the carriage. "How about we drop the subject so everyone can eat in peace."

"He started it." Hal glared at Mervyn Crosby. He was so angry he was trembling.

Mervyn Crosby laughed meanly.

"Now, boy," said Mr. Ackerman with a sickly smile, "let's not ruin everyone's evening with petty accusations."

"Don't think that I don't *know* why you're sucking up to Mr. Crosby," Hal replied, glaring at Mr. Ackerman.

"Whatever do you mean?" Mr. Ackerman laughed nervously.

"Hal," Uncle Nat said, a note of warning in his voice.

"I saw you taking money from that man back in the station. It was a bribe, wasn't it?"

There were gasps, and Hal could feel he had the attention of everyone in the room. He pulled out his sketchbook and opened it to the picture of Luther Ackerman receiving the money. He held it up.

"And later, you were heard on the phone, making special arrangements with someone called Mr. Leon—I have a witness. Was it him who paid you to let Mr. Crosby shoot a rhino from the train?"

There was a long silence, filled only by Hal's own heavy breathing.

"Oh dear, you've let your imagination run away with you." Luther Ackerman spoke calmly but coldly. "I do not need to explain myself to you, child, but Mr. Crosby and I spoke in private earlier this evening about how I would *not* let him hunt from the train. I told him of some hunting reserves he might enjoy visiting once we arrive in Zambia. I even gave him brochures, did I not, Mr. Crosby?"

"Sure did." Mr. Crosby nodded.

"The special arrangements you heard me discussing with Mr. Leon were for another guest."

"They were for me," said Portia Ramaboa. "Mr. Leon is my dietician—I have allergies." She smiled apologetically at Hal, and his stomach lurched.

"I'm sorry to be discussing this publicly, Ms. Ramaboa," Mr. Ackerman said, shooting Hal a sour look.

Portia waved her hand. "It's nothing."

"Not that it's any concern of yours, but the man in your little drawing is Enzo, and I wasn't *taking* money from him. As you can clearly see in your picture, I was *giving* him money. He's a supplier of locomotive parts. I have to source them from specialists. They're not cheap, and scrap merchants only take cash." He paused. "I know you like to play at being a detective, child, but I think perhaps this time your game has gone too far. Please apologize to Mr. Crosby and Ms. Ramaboa so we can all get back to enjoying our dinner."

Hal's mouth had gone dry. He opened it to speak, but nothing came out.

Mervyn Crosby put his hand to his ear. "I can't hear you."

"I'm sorry, Mr. Crosby. I'm sorry, Ms. Ramaboa," Hal mumbled.

"What was that?" Mervyn Crosby said, grinning.

"You heard him perfectly well, Mr. Crosby," Uncle Nat said, giving Hal a sympathetic look. "Sit down, Hal."

Hal did as he was told, burning with shame.

Satsuki Sasaki pulled his sketchbook across the table, turning to the back, and looked at him for permission to tear out a blank page. He nodded. She folded the thin paper and carefully ripped off a rectangle to make a perfect square. Uncle Nat fell into conversation with Ryo as Hal watched Satsuki's nimble fingers turning the paper, folding it expertly. She pushed the paper along the creases, forming flaps, each movement more intricate than the last. Hal was entranced by her speed and certainty, trying to work out what she was making. He thought it was a ship, because the paper curved like the hull of a boat, but then she turned it around and he realized he'd been looking at the back of it.

"An owl," she said, standing it on the table in front of him, "for luck."

"For me?" Hal was touched.

Satsuki nodded. "When I feel bad, origami makes me calm, and I see solutions."

"That's like drawing, for me." Hal smiled, grateful for her kindness.

***

Once they were back in their compartment, Uncle Nat sat him down. "Are you all right?"

"I'm fine," Hal lied, shame smoldering inside him. "I don't understand how I got it so wrong."

"You shouldn't have let Mervyn Crosby goad you into losing your temper like that. If you'd taken the time to learn more, you'd have found out who Mr. Leon was. You know better than anyone that there's a difference between having a lead and having proof."

Uncle Nat shook his head, and Hal thought he was about to

be told off, but instead Uncle Nat said, "He really is the most odious man."

"Aren't you cross with me?"

"Luther Ackerman punished you enough with that public humiliation without me adding to it." Uncle Nat sighed.

"The safari tomorrow is going to be awful," Hal said miserably. "Everyone thinks I'm a stupid child."

"Nonsense. First, I don't imagine Luther will be going, and, second, other than his wife and daughter, I don't think there's a soul on this train who wouldn't be happier if Mr. Crosby wasn't here. I'm sure you'll discover that everyone is on your side."

Uncle Nat's words made Hal feel better, but the thought of the scene in the dining car made his face burn anew. He was glad Winston hadn't been there to witness his humiliation. He wished Erik Lovejoy had been absent, too—he wanted to impress the retired detective.

"We should turn in," Uncle Nat said, taking off his jacket. "We've got an early start tomorrow."

Hal climbed into bed and stared at the world outside the window. It had become a shadowland of silhouettes; the Drakensberg mountains lay like vast sleeping dragons under a star-speckled midnight sky. He looked down again at his picture of Luther Ackerman. Had he been wrong about the money changing hands? He didn't think so.

CHAPTER EIGHT

PIPER AT THE GATES OF DAWN

Hal was awake, staring at the ceiling of the carriage, when the alarm chirped on one of Uncle Nat's watches. He'd had a restless night, waking when the train stopped moving and not able to get back to sleep. The events of the previous night had repeated themselves in his dreams. He'd made a mistake, accusing Mr. Ackerman without proof. He'd been momentarily shaken by the man's cool response, but he was certain the story about Enzo wasn't true. He decided to ask Flo about the spare-parts dealer when he saw her. Sitting up, he peered through the wooden blind. The Safari Star had stopped in a siding outside Hoedspruit station. The world was bathed in a dark sapphire light, and not even the sun was up yet.

Uncle Nat fumbled with his watch to turn off the alarm and groaned as he patted the thin table between their beds, feeling for his glasses.

"Morning," Hal whispered.

Pulling on the long khaki shorts and fawn polo shirt his mom had bought him to wear on safari, Hal felt a thrill of excitement as he wondered what animals he would see that day.

Once they were dressed and ready, Uncle Nat led the way out of the compartment. The thought of spending the day with Mervyn Crosby was tying Hal's stomach in knots, but he wasn't going to let the man ruin his first-ever safari.

Stepping down from the train was like entering another world. The dusty ground glimmered with dawn dew, and the air was cool, full of the raucous chatter of birds. Hal's sneakers crunched on the ballast as he walked toward the loco where Liana Tsotsobe was waiting for them, hands on her hips. As the sleepy passengers stumbled toward Liana, Hal saw that everyone was wearing safari colors, except Beryl Brash, who was dressed in a plum-colored kaftan robe, and Mervyn Crosby, who was wearing another pink shirt under his safari jacket.

"Good morning," said Liana. "Today we explore a small part of Kruger National Park, one of the wildlife wonders of South Africa. This early, you'll see nocturnal animals settling down to rest, as other animals wake. Be quiet, respectful, and follow our instructions." She spoke like a teacher whom nobody would dare disobey.

"We will be dividing into two groups. I shall guide one, and Darren will look after the other."

A man with a ginger beard and a green cap pulled down over his eyes stepped forward and nodded at them.

"Darren is a ranger from Kruger National Park. It's an hour's drive to the Orpen Gate. We've already been on the radio to get an update on animal sightings." She scanned the group, stopping when she found Mervyn Crosby. "We will be doing a mandatory bag check as you get in the Jeeps. You are not permitted to carry weapons."

Mervyn Crosby snorted.

"You will see park sightings boards once we're through the gate. These won't include information on rhinos. Sadly, the park loses a rhino a day to illegal poachers, so their locations are not reported. If you are fortunate enough to see a rhino, you must not tell anyone where you saw it. This is for the safety of the animals." Liana smiled. "Okay, down this path are two Jeeps. My son, Winston, will lead you to them."

She pointed, and Winston waved from the path. Hal waved back at him.

"Let's go," Liana said.

Beryl clutched at Erik's arm. "You're such a gentleman," she said, smiling up at him. "A lady could have a nasty fall on a path like this."

The path through the gnarled and leafless trees was completely flat, and Hal grinned as he ran ahead to join Winston and Chipo.

"I heard about you accusing Mr. Ackerman last night," Winston whispered. "That was a bold move."

"Urgh, it was awful," Hal said, blushing as he realized the train crew must have been talking about it for Winston to know. "Can you try to make sure I'm not put in the same group as Mr. Crosby today, please?"

"No problem."

The path led to a clearing where two enormous Jeeps with tarpaulin roofs were parked behind a trestle table covered with pastries, breads, meats, cheese, and fruit, as well as cold bottles of water and fruit juice.

"Help yourselves to breakfast," Liana called out. "We will eat on the road."

As they filled their paper bags, Winston watched Amelia Crosby take a seat in one of the Jeeps. He nudged Hal, and they promptly grabbed their drinks and made their way to the other vehicle.

The Jeep had three rows of three seats, each row set a little higher than the one in front. As they climbed into the middle row, Chipo

jumped off Winston's shoulder. Hal saw her run back to the breakfast table and leap up beside a bowl of nuts, where Mervyn Crosby was filling a roll with sliced meat.

"Chipo!" Winston hissed. "Come back here, girl!"

Mervyn Crosby jumped and bellowed when he saw Chipo, slapping her off the table with the back of his hand.

Hal gasped as the startled mongoose tumbled to the ground.

"*No!*" Winston cried out as Mervyn Crosby drew back his foot, aiming a vicious kick at her.

But before he could strike, Uncle Nat jumped in front of Chipo, and Mr. Crosby's boot connected hard with his ankle. Uncle Nat gasped with the pain and sank to the ground.

"Uncle Nat!" Hal scrambled out of the Jeep, running over. "Are you okay?"

"Chipo!" Winston whistled, and the frightened mongoose scampered to his side.

"You idiot!" Mervyn barked at Uncle Nat. "What are you doing?"

Erik put a firm hand on Mr. Crosby's arm and said in a reasonable voice, "Mr. Crosby, you've just assaulted Nathaniel Bradshaw in front of witnesses. If I were you, I would be apologizing, not shouting at him."

"That giant rat was after my food!" Mervyn Crosby's nostrils flared with indignation as he shook off Erik's grip.

"The creature is a tame yellow mongoose," said Uncle Nat, gritting his teeth at the pain he was in.

"It meant no harm," he said, as Hal helped him to his feet.

"Dumb Brit," Mr. Crosby muttered.

Erik bristled. "You may not have any manners, Mr. Crosby, but you're not above the law."

"That's where you're wrong." Mervyn Crosby leaned down so that his nose was almost touching Erik's. "There isn't any court in any country that would dare try to prosecute me." He grinned, then stalked away to the other Jeep to join his wife.

Nicole Crosby looked at Hal apologetically. She seemed to be about to say something, but she gave a little shake of her head and followed her dad with her shoulders slumped and her head hanging low.

"Not a humane bone in his body." Erik looked at Nat apologetically.

"I thought you were masterful," Beryl said.

"I'll get your breakfast for you," Hal said as he helped Uncle Nat hop to the Jeep.

"Oh, Mr. Bradshaw, thank you," said Winston, cuddling Chipo. "A kick like that could have killed her. I owe you."

"You owe me nothing, Winston," Uncle Nat said with a pained smile. "I was just protecting a harmless animal from a dangerous one."

Liana took over, sitting Uncle Nat on the back row of the Jeep's seats, so he could stretch his leg out along them. She bandaged his ankle and propped it up on an ice pack. "I'm going to put your boot back on, but not tie it tightly. It will help reduce the swelling."

"I'm fine, really," Uncle Nat protested.

"You'll have a nasty bruise, but it isn't a sprain. Once the swelling's gone down, you should be able to walk."

"You okay?" Erik asked, passing Uncle Nat a flask of coffee as Hal clambered in next to Winston. "Got yourself a whole row of seats, I see."

"We'll just have to bunch up in the front, Erik," said Beryl, clambering in and patting the seat next to hers.

"So we will," said Erik, giving Uncle Nat a *This is your fault* look.

"Is that everyone?" asked Liana, climbing into the driver's seat.

"Wait!" Nicole Crosby ran up to their vehicle. Her fists were clenched. "Can I come with you?" She looked like she might cry. "Please?"

"Sure." Hal shifted up to make room for her.

"Thanks." Nicole wiped her face with her sleeve as she climbed up and sat next to him.

Liana turned the key in the ignition. "Eat your breakfast. Have a nap if you're sleepy." She put the Jeep into gear and reversed onto the dirt track that led to the highway. "It's safari time."

As they passed the other Jeep, Hal felt a wave of joy to be driving away from Mervyn Crosby. He stiffened, thinking that Portia Ramaboa was gazing at him but then realized it wasn't him she was looking at. "Nicole, Portia Ramaboa's staring at you."

Nicole turned and smiled at her. "She's cool." As the distance between the two vehicles widened, Nicole turned to face Uncle Nat. "I'm really sorry about your ankle. I hope it doesn't ruin your safari."

"It's very kind of you to apologize," said Uncle Nat, "but you haven't done anything wrong, and nothing's going to ruin today."

"Pop's the worst," she blurted out. "I hate him."

"I'm sure he's not that bad," Hal said, not believing what he was saying.

"He is. But I won't have to put up with him for much longer—I'm almost seventeen." Nicole's face was set. "I'm going to move to the other side of the States, to go to college, and then I won't have to see him." She looked at Hal. "You were brave to stand up to him last night. I've seen him make grown men cry."

"Oh, yes," Beryl chipped in, "it was adorable when you played detective. I only wish that you'd been right. It was such a shame that you ended up with egg on your face."

Her words stung, but Hal forced a smile and tried to look like he didn't mind.

"Don't beat yourself up about it," Erik said. "If you're going to be a detective, you'll make plenty of mistakes. I've made thousands." He paused. "Do you have your sketchbook with you? I wanted to take a look at your picture."

"Of course," Hal said, feeling a glow of gratitude at Erik's words. He pulled his book from his bag and passed it forward.

Erik stared at the picture, gave a curt nod, and handed it back. "Thanks."

Hal exchanged glances with Winston, but the retired detective didn't say anything more.

The sun rose in the sky, bathing the passing farmland in a mellow, citrus-pink light. Hal felt the soft wind buffeting his face and drew in a deep breath, smiling. Uncle Nat was right. Nothing could ruin the day. He was going on safari.

CHAPTER NINE

ON SAFARI

An hour later, they passed through the Orpen Gate into Kruger National Park, and Liana pulled the Jeep over to the side of the road. Picking up the radio receiver, she held down a button and asked for an update, then listened intently. Beryl was snoring gently, cuddled up to Erik, using his shoulder as a pillow. He was sitting bolt upright, wide awake.

The other Jeep passed them, and Nicole slouched down in her seat at the same time as Hal did. They both laughed.

"We're in luck," Liana called over her shoulder. "A pride of lions has brought down a water buffalo not far from here. Want to see them eating breakfast?" She looked at Hal and Nicole. "I'm warning you—it will not be a pretty sight." They nodded to show they understood.

The Jeep moved through the park at a sedate pace. The ground was rocky, the grass dry, and many of the trees looked dead. Hal scanned the landscape for wildlife, trying to remember his geography lessons on the savanna. As the sun rose, so did the temperature, and he took off his fleece, applying sunscreen to his face and neck.

Tapping him on the shoulder, Uncle Nat pointed to the high branches of a tree. As the Jeep rolled past, Hal saw a pair of birds with cinnamon-pink breasts, black-and-white-striped wings, long dark beaks, and crowns of pink feathers that rose like mohawks.

Nicole lifted her phone and snapped a photograph.

"Hoopoes," whispered Winston.

"I do," Hal whispered back. "Don't you poo, too?"

Winston giggled and Nicole rolled her eyes.

"*Elephants!*" Beryl shrieked, standing up and falling back into her seat. "Look! And *baby* ones!"

Liana stopped the car as a herd of elephants lumbered across the road. One paused to peel a branch from a tree with its trunk, sticking it in its mouth like a lollipop and stripping the leaves.

"Oh, where's my camera?" Beryl said to herself as she fumbled in her handbag. She found it and shoved it at Erik before striking a pose, pointing at the elephant and beaming while he took pictures.

Hal used his charcoal to draw the curve of the elephant's back and the cheerful curl of its trunk. He shaded its folds of thick hide and added a scrappy little tail with a flourish. The impressive animal was only yards away. He was so intently focused on drawing it he forgot to breathe. The wonder of being in South Africa, sketching a real elephant, hit him with full force, and he found he was grinning as uncontrollably as Beryl.

"African elephants can talk to each other over huge distances," Winston said. "But their voices are so low humans can't hear them."

"Elephants talk?" Beryl looked delighted and whispered to herself. "*Nature's great masterpiece.*"

"Beautiful." Nicole sighed.

"Big *is* beautiful." Beryl winked at Erik.

"That's your first of the Big Five," Uncle Nat said, leaning forward to admire Hal's sketch. "Very good."

"We're not far from where the lions brought down that water buffalo," Liana said, as the elephant marched off to catch up with the others. "When we get there, you must all stay inside the vehicle. Big cats are dangerous."

Hal was excited and nervous about seeing the lions, but he wasn't prepared for the sight that greeted them down the road. A dead buffalo was splayed in an awkward position on the ground, looking like a wrecked ship with its hull torn away. Four lionesses were sitting around it, calmly and slowly ripping meat from the carcass, their mouths smeared red and pink. Hal stared, rigid with shock. The buffalo was empty of life, but the lionesses were electrifyingly vivid.

"Are you okay?" He felt Uncle Nat's hand on his shoulder, and Hal nodded, unable to speak. Tears were pricking the backs of his eyes.

"'Nature, red in tooth and claw,'" Uncle Nat said quietly as Hal's charcoal moved across the sketchbook.

"Tennyson," Beryl said, nodding at Uncle Nat.

Hal knew this was the way wild animals lived and ate. He'd seen many TV programs where animals hunted other animals. *I am lucky to be seeing this*, he thought, as he drew. *This is life, and death. This is real.*

"'Nature, red in tooth and claw,'" Nicole repeated, and Hal heard the click of her camera.

"Clever hyena," Winston murmured, pointing to a smudge,

a black nose and two button eyes, hiding in the grass beneath a wide-canopied tree, "waits patiently for a buffalo breakfast."

"Here comes trouble." Liana motioned behind them. The elephants they'd been admiring up the road were marching toward the lions, increasing their pace, with their trunks raised. "This is elephant territory. They won't welcome the lions. We'd better move on."

They all turned to watch the elephants chase the lions away from their breakfast as the Jeep drove off and, sure enough, moments later the hyena stole out of the long grass and tore a strip from the buffalo.

"That was *thrilling*," said Beryl, fanning herself. "It was so . . . so raw, so wild."

"Life is brutal," agreed Erik.

"I think we have had enough drama, yes?" Liana asked. "Let's find the elephants' watering hole and see who is welcome there."

The Jeep rumbled over the lumpy ground toward a wide pool of water crowded with creatures gathering for a morning drink. A cluster of storks with red-and-yellow beaks landed with a graceless splash, and a baby elephant—small enough to fit underneath its mother's belly—stumbled into the water, flapping its ears in delight.

They stopped about ten yards away, and Liana switched off the engine. "We can get out if you like. Nothing here will harm you as long as you are respectful and keep your distance. Stick to the path. Do not walk into the bush."

"I think I'll stay here," Uncle Nat said. "My leg still feels a little tender."

Following Winston out of the Jeep, Hal pointed out a herd of

black-and-white horned animals, part horse, part goat, drinking at the water's edge.

"Sable antelope," Winston whispered. "I'm going to get a bit closer."

Hal wasn't keen to get too close to the animals, but he wanted a good angle to draw from. He saw a barren tree with a large rock in front of it that he could lean his pad on and headed over.

He drew the shape of the shimmering watering hole and paused to enjoy the playful games of the monkeys splashing about at the water's edge. His charcoal danced and skipped as he worked to get their outlines. Once he had them, he lifted his binoculars to see their faces more clearly. Turning the dial to focus the lenses, he noticed a dark shape in the distance, moving above the savanna grasses. He stepped back from the rock, leaning against the tree trunk as the image came into focus. He gasped. It was a black rhino, traveling alone on the far side of the watering hole. The rhino's horn was missing—it had only a stump. Hal heard the distant exclamations from the rest of the group as they saw it, too. He lowered his binoculars. The rhino was still too far away to have upset the drinking animals, but one or two lifted their heads, alerted by the sound of its approach.

Something touched Hal's right shoulder. He turned his head. From the corner of his eye, he saw a silvery gray snake's head, sliding from the tree trunk onto him, moving toward his neck. With a cold flash of horror, he realized he'd disobeyed Liana and strayed from the path.

"Help," he squeaked, frozen with fear. "Uncle Nat!" But Uncle Nat was in the Jeep, and too far away to hear him.

CHAPTER TEN

THE BLACK MAMBA

Don't move." Erik Lovejoy's voice was calm and commanding. Hal couldn't breathe. The snake's head was hanging over his right shoulder. He could feel the weight of its body, and his heart was beating so hard he felt it might burst out of his chest.

"Keep very still."

The snake's shifting coils touched the back of his neck. It was cold and smooth. Hal heard a rustle and the sound of breaking sticks. He felt a sharp jab to his shoulder blade, and for one terrifying moment thought he'd been bitten, but then the weight of the snake's body shifted. It became lighter and was gone.

Hal saw Erik step away, holding two sticks out at arm's length. One had a forked end from which the snake's head rose, the second stick was stuck through the coil of the snake's body. Slowly and gently, Erik lowered the sticks to the ground, dropping them before swiftly stepping sideways to Hal. He put his arm round Hal's shoulder.

"Step backward with me. And again, and again."

Hal felt the firm path under his feet, and his knees went to jelly. He leaned against Erik as the snake slithered away into the undergrowth.

"Were you bitten?"

Hal shook his head. "Thank you," he whispered.

Winston was running toward them, looking at Erik in awe. "That was a . . ."

"A black mamba." Erik nodded. "I know."

"A black mamba?" Hal was shaking.

"It's one of the deadliest snakes in the world," said Winston, his eyes wide. "Its venom paralyzes you so it can eat you alive."

Hal's legs buckled, but Erik grabbed his arm and put it over his shoulder, half carrying Hal back to the Jeep.

"Hal?" Uncle Nat was clambering out of the vehicle.

"He's okay," Erik called out. "He's not hurt."

"What is going on?" asked Liana, running to them.

"Mr. Lovejoy saved Hal from a black mamba!" Winston told his mother.

"Do you have any water?" Erik asked as Beryl hurried over. "He's in shock."

"Here." Beryl took a sweet from her handbag, unwrapped it, and popped it into Hal's mouth. "It's a butterscotch. It'll help." She smiled encouragingly at Hal, then looked adoringly at Erik. "You are a hero, Mr. Lovejoy."

Uncle Nat limped toward them, clutching a canteen of water. He drew Hal into a hug. "Thank goodness you're okay! I should have got out of the Jeep with you. Erik, thank you. I don't know what to say . . . I'd never have forgiven myself if . . ."

"You'd have done the same," Erik said dismissively.

Liana gently chided Hal for stepping off the path while Uncle

Nat helped him up into the back
row of the Jeep. He hung Hal's
fleece round his shoulders, encouraging
him to drink more water. Hal's head was spinning.
He was shaking, and he couldn't get the image of the dead
buffalo out of his head.

Nicole sat down in front of Hal. "Did you see the
rhino?" she whispered. "It was beautiful. I got some great
pictures of it."

Hal tried to smile and nod.

"If everyone is finished here, I think we should move on," Liana said. "Back to your seats."

As the Jeep bounced away from the watering hole, Hal looked out across the parkland and saw the world anew. For the first time in his life he appreciated how powerful and deadly nature could be.

They rendezvoused at an appointed clearing for lunch. The others were already there, parked beside a foldaway table covered with trays of sandwiches and fruit in the shade of wide-canopied trees.

Winston needed only a little coaxing from Beryl to launch into the story of Hal's encounter with the black mamba, describing the snake as being bigger and angrier than Hal remembered it. Beryl leaped in to describe Erik's heroic rescue and how he'd carried Hal in his arms back to the Jeep.

Uncle Nat chuckled, but Hal shook his head. That was twice he'd managed to look like an idiot in front of everyone on the train. He'd wanted this journey to be like his other two with his uncle, but instead, so far, he'd invented a crime and nearly been bitten by a venomous snake. The only thing that made him feel better was that Erik was looking as uncomfortable as he felt about the story Beryl and Winston were telling. And then suddenly a cold flood of dismay washed through him as he realized he'd left his sketchbook on the rock by the watering hole.

"You okay?" Uncle Nat asked him for the thousandth time.

"Yeah." Hal nodded, forcing a smile. "I'm going to get some more sandwiches." He made a show of going to the table, but all he was thinking about was his sketchbook. He couldn't ask Liana to drive all the way back for it. Everyone would think he was a baby for making a fuss—he just had to accept that it was gone. A yawning hollow feeling opened up inside him, and he sighed. The journey wasn't turning out to be the adventure he'd hoped for. He picked up an apple, deciding to stop searching for crimes and concentrate on the good things about the holiday.

Winston was sitting in the shade of a baobab tree with a plate of sandwiches on his lap.

"Can I join you?" Hal asked.

"Don't worry. Chipo's here to protect you from snakes," Winston said, nodding.

Hal laughed bitterly, thinking he was being mocked.

"I'm serious! The only animal that can fight a black mamba and live is Chipo. The yellow mongoose is a natural snake hunter. She's resistant to their venom."

"Really?" Hal looked at Chipo, who stared blankly at him. She didn't look like a snake wrestler.

"Yes, and she does tricks." Winston took two peanuts from his plate. "Watch this." He threw a nut high above his head, catching it in his open mouth as it fell, then he flicked the second one skyward, and snapped his fingers. Chipo jumped, snatching the nut out of the air and landing neatly on his left shoulder. She stuffed the peanut into her mouth.

Hal clapped and laughed.

"Hi." The boys looked up as Nicole walked over. "They're clearing lunch away. Mrs. Sasaki has asked to be taken back to the train—she's tired. Your mom said Hal's uncle should go, too, to rest his ankle. She's going to drive them, but because there are only two Jeeps, we have to continue the safari in the other one."

She paused. "I've decided to go back to the train, too. I don't want to go with Pop."

"I'll come with you, to help Uncle Nat," Hal said, getting to his feet. The thought of being stuck with Mervyn Crosby all afternoon wasn't appealing, and he was still feeling shaky after his run-in with the snake.

"I can't take Chipo in a Jeep with Mr. Crosby." Winston jumped up. "I'm coming, too. Hey, do you want to help me make Chipo a run?"

"What's a run?" Hal asked.

"It's a system of tunnels. Mongooses love tunnels."

"Sounds fun."

"Can I help?" Nicole asked.

"Of course." Winston nodded. "The bigger the run, the happier Chipo will be."

***

An hour later, as their Jeep drove up to the Safari Star, Janice's green flank glinted in the sunlight and they saw Flo Ackerman standing on the top of the tender, guiding the wide nozzle of a water pipe into a hatch to refill the tank. She waved when she saw them.

"Who's that?" Nicole asked as they got out of the Jeep.

"Flo Ackerman. She's the train engineer," Hal replied. "She's really cool."

"Ha! Pop would blow a fuse if he knew the person in charge of our train was a woman."

"I need to ask her something," Hal said, mournfully thinking of his sketchbook sitting on the rock back at the watering hole as he ran to the tender.

"Hey, Flo," he called up. "What's the name of the person you get your specialist steam-engine parts from?"

The sun was high, and it was an instant relief to be standing out of the day's heat in the train's shadow.

Flo looked surprised by the question. "We get them from this scrap dealer called Enzo," she called back. "Why?"

"Oh, nothing, just a conversation me and Uncle Nat were having," Hal replied, feeling disappointed. "Thanks."

He followed Winston and Nicole to an empty compartment in the service cars. Heaving a duffel bag off the bottom bunk, Winston pulled out twenty old poster tubes, a handful of black socks, and a roll of gaffer tape.

"Your socks are missing their toes," said Nicole, putting her hand right through one.

"I cut them off," Winston explained, as Hal peered through one of the tubes like a telescope. "The socks connect the tubes. You put the sock over the end of the tube, tape it up, then insert the next tube into the sock and tape around that. You keep going until you have a really long tunnel with bends in."

"You don't have junctions?" Hal asked.

"'Course I do," Winston scoffed. "Chipo has to have more than one tunnel to choose from."

"What do you use to make the junction?" Nicole asked.

"Diapers!" Winston yanked a handful from an outside pocket of the duffel bag.

"You're so weird." Nicole giggled.

The three of them got to work on the run, while Chipo leaped about excitedly, zooming through tubes and making it more of a challenge.

Winston put a sock over his hand and chased Hal around the cabin pretending it was a snake, as Hal shrieked, "Save me, Erik!"

Nicole resisted for a moment, obviously feeling she was too old for such a game, but then grabbed a poster tube and laughed as she whacked Winston's hand, shouting "Die, snake, die!" and they fell about laughing.

"Winston, that rhino in the park, why didn't it have a horn?" Nicole asked, as she fixed a vertical tube to the bunk bed ladder.

"The park owners will have taken it off," said Winston, taping a sock to another tube. "The poachers won't want to kill the rhino if there's no horn to steal. It's a way of keeping rhinos alive. They put the rhino to sleep with a dart and saw it off. It doesn't hurt. It's like cutting your nails."

"I've tried to talk to Pop about hunting a million times." Nicole gave them a grim smile. "He thinks I hate it because I'm a 'sensitive girl.'"

"Your dad is a difficult person to like," Hal admitted.

"Are you still investigating Mr. Ackerman?" Winston asked Hal.

Hal shook his head. "I got that wrong."

"I thought you were onto something." Winston looked disappointed.

"Who needs a crime to solve? The Safari Star is brilliant. South Africa is amazing," said Hal.

Chipo sat up and squeaked.

"Yes, Chipo, the wildlife is cool, too."

They all laughed.

"Anyway, I left my sketchbook back at the watering hole." He shrugged. "I don't think I could solve a crime without it."

"Oh no! All your pictures!" Winston said. "What are you going to draw in now?"

Hal shrugged and changed the subject. "How's the run coming along?"

"It's finished," Winston said, fastening a bit of tape round the rim of a sock. "That's the last tube. The mongoose run is officially open!"

He took his hand away from the opening, and Chipo zipped in, rocketing through the tubes. The run started on the floor, climbed to the bottom bunk, running flat to the window, moving vertically to the luggage rack, where it split into a high circle around the ceiling and made a path back down again. Chipo hared round it again and again in delight.

They heard the crackle of tires skidding in the dirt and all looked out of the window. The other Jeep was back.

"It must be four o'clock," Winston said.

"Time for high tea," said Nicole, and they shared a disappointed look at the thought of rejoining the adults.

CHAPTER ELEVEN

HIGH DOH!

The whistle of the Safari Star was followed by the *huff, huff, huff* of smoke being expelled from her chimney and the compressed hiss of pistons turning her giant wheels, as the towering locomotive heaved her carriages away from Hoedspruit, northward through the savanna.

Hal arrived at the door of the observation car flanked by Winston and Nicole. The train was traveling at such a slow speed it would've pleased Queen Victoria. The horizon was all hills, although they might have been mountains—Hal couldn't judge the distance.

Uncle Nat was sitting with Erik at a nearby table, chuckling at a joke. He smiled when he saw them enter. "Hal, Erik has something for you."

Hal shuffled forward, suddenly bashful. "Mr. Lovejoy, I don't think I thanked you properly for saving my life."

"*Psht!*" Erik waved his hand. "I didn't save your life. I took a snake off you, that's all. It wasn't going to bite you." He was being kind. Hal knew from everyone's reaction that he'd been in real danger. "Anyway, after I handed you over to your uncle, I went

91

back and got this." He pushed Hal's sketchbook across the table.

Overwhelmed to see it again, Hal swallowed hard and blinked back the sudden tears. "Thank you," he whispered, picking it up and clutching it to his chest.

"I took a look at the sketches you did in Kruger Park. You've got an eye for detail. I'm not surprised you're a good detective."

Hal blushed at the praise, and Uncle Nat smiled proudly.

"Oh no," Nicole muttered.

Amelia Crosby, who'd spotted her daughter enter, was tottering over in high heels.

"Hi, Mom," Nicole said brightly.

"Nic, your father wants to talk to you." Amelia looked anxious.

"I'm hanging with these guys. I'll talk to him later."

"Really?" Amelia looked at Hal and Winston as if she'd never seen them before. "Bit young to be your friends, aren't they?"

"You don't get to choose who my friends are." Nicole folded her arms.

"Look, you know it's not a good idea to make your father wait. That Ramaboa woman's got him all stirred up. On the safari, she told him that you were exceptionally bright and that he should be supporting your ambition to go to college. How does she know that you want to go to college?" The look on Amelia's face was panicked.

"I told her," Nicole replied defiantly, but she followed her mother across the carriage, pausing to look back and roll her eyes at Hal and Winston.

Beryl made a grand entrance wearing an elaborate hat with a brim so wide it got wedged in the doorway. "Heavens!" she exclaimed as she wobbled it free. "The price one pays for fashion."

She slumped into an armchair by the door, extracting a notepad and fountain pen from her handbag. She smiled at Erik and fluttered her eyelashes, then began scribbling intently in her book.

"Time for me to make my escape," Erik said in a low voice. He fiddled with his watch, then announced loudly, "Oh, is that the time! I'm sorry, Nat, I have some important business to take care of in my compartment." He got up. "I shall see you at dinner."

Hal slipped into his seat, and Winston pulled over another chair. "I bet the hero of Beryl's next book is Erik Lovejoy," Hal whispered, and they giggled.

"No!" Mervyn Crosby's objection silenced the observation lounge. Everyone looked toward the veranda. "I'll sponsor the sports team or buy them a building, but no daughter of mine is taking tests like a pleb."

"They're entrance exams, Pop, and I want to take them."

"You don't need to go to college." Mervyn Crosby thumped his chest. "Your pop's rich." Amelia was sitting beside him, staring blankly at the floor.

"I'm going to study business management at Harvard," Nicole said obstinately.

"You don't need to go to college to understand business," Mervyn Crosby huffed. "I didn't. You start at the bottom and work your way up. I can get you a nice job as a secretary at one of my companies."

"I don't want to work for you," Nicole snapped. "I want to set up my own business." Her eyes darted around the room, and connected with those of Portia Ramaboa, who nodded.

"I'll set up a business for you. What do you want to sell? Makeup? You'd be good at that. You're pretty." He broke off a bit of cake and tossed it at his mouth. It missed, bouncing off his chin and rolling down his pink shirt.

"You're not listening to me." Nicole was losing her temper. "I *am* going to go to Harvard, whether you like it or not."

"If I don't like it, you're not going."

"Urghhh!" she shrieked. "You're ruining my life!" She pushed back her chair and stormed out of the carriage.

"Nic, Nic, come back," Amelia called, chasing after her daughter.

There was a long silence.

"You should support your daughter, not stifle her," Portia said from across the carriage. "You will regret it if you don't."

"Shut up, woman," replied Mervyn Crosby.

"Don't speak to her like that." Patrice Mbatha spun round in his chair.

"I'll speak to her any way I choose." Mr. Crosby stuck out his chin.

"You're a bad man, Mr. Crosby," Patrice said, rising to stand. "Rotten through and through." He threw his napkin down on the table. "You are rude and objectionable. You kicked Mr. Bradshaw this morning and didn't offer a word of apology." He gestured to Uncle Nat. "You talked about the beautiful animals we saw in the park like a butcher. You don't care if you're upsetting people or ruining their holiday." He shook his head. "People put up with you because you're wealthy, but I will not. You are a monster."

"Who are you again?" Mervyn Crosby said, looking unimpressed. "Patrick, was it?"

"You know who I am."

"I meet hundreds of people, thousands every year." He stared blankly at Patrice. "I only remember the important ones."

Patrice clenched his fists. Hal thought he was going to explode, but instead he turned and marched out of the carriage.

Mervyn Crosby laughed. "You'll want to get yourself a new boyfriend," he said as Portia got up. "That one's a loser, a total drip."

Portia fixed Mr. Crosby with a look so fierce that Hal suddenly felt nervous.

"Karma is a boomerang, Mr. Crosby. One way or another, we get what we deserve." She followed Patrice out of the room.

Beryl muttered to herself, and her scribbling intensified.

Mervyn Crosby seemed unperturbed by the drama he'd caused and helped himself to another cake.

"Look!" Winston pointed out the window. Thick rows of maize danced past like a swaying chorus line.

A herd of wild impalas was grazing beside the track. Spooked by the noise of the train, they'd started running and were picking up speed.

With his sketchbook clutched to his chest, Hal ran past Mr. Crosby to the veranda. Pulling his tin of charcoal from his trouser pocket, he leaned on the brass railing, thrilled to be able to draw in the book he thought he'd lost. He sketched dark eyes, crowned with a pair of demonic-looking horns. The sweeping line of the impala's back, moving down to the muscular haunches of the back legs. They were so close that Hal thought he might be able to touch one.

"They're as fast as the train," Uncle Nat said from behind him.

"Impala can run up to ninety kilometers an hour," Winston replied. "But they zigzag, see? To avoid being caught by predators."

"It'd be fun to shoot one down." Mervyn Crosby had followed them out onto the veranda. He pointed two fingers at them. "*Pow.*"

Hal looked at Uncle Nat in alarm.

"Isn't it more wonderful for them to be alive, to see them running in their natural habitat?" Uncle Nat asked patiently.

"Nah, that's boring. It's exhilarating to chase 'em and shoot 'em."

"You wouldn't shoot a human for fun, so why an animal?" Hal asked.

"What makes you think I wouldn't shoot a human?" Mr. Crosby leered at Hal.

"We're not scared of you," Winston said, standing beside Hal. "You're a bully, and my mama says all bullies are cowards."

"You *should* be scared of me. Didn't you hear what that Patrick guy said? I'm a monster." Mr. Crosby gave a great gurgling laugh and leaned out, looking toward the front of the train. He did a double take. His eyes lit up, and he grabbed at the pair of binoculars hanging around his neck. "Well, I'll be damned, it's the very place," he muttered, checking his watch, then hurrying back into the observation car with a wicked grin.

Winston and Hal looked at each other, alarmed, and followed him.

"Where are you going?" Hal called out.

"You don't want to know, little boy." He grinned over his shoulder. "It might give you nightmares."

"You're not going to shoot at the impala?" Hal pleaded.

"Firing guns from the train is dangerous. My mama—" Winston began.

"Listen, kid, I don't give a hill of beans for anything your mama says. And, no, I'm not going to shoot an impala—I've killed hundreds." He pointed. "I'm gonna shoot the rhino I just saw."

"*What?*" Hal and Winston spun round, craning their necks to look as Mr. Crosby hurried away.

"Uncle Nat!" Hal cried. "Quick, Mr. Crosby's going to shoot a rhino from the train!" All three of them dashed into the sleeping car.

"He's in the Royal Suite," said Uncle Nat. "That door." He hammered his fist against it. "Mr. Crosby! You must not fire your gun from the train. Do you hear me?" He tried the handle. It was locked. "Mr. Crosby, I'll fetch Mr. Ackerman if you—"

"Go get him!" Mr. Crosby called out. "See if I care."

Uncle Nat looked at Hal. "He's got a gun in there. I don't want you anywhere near it. Go back and sit in the observation car. I'm going to get Mr. Ackerman."

Hal nodded, as Uncle Nat hobbled away down the corridor.

"Come on." Winston yanked his sleeve.

Hal heard Mr. Crosby slide his window down with a click and thought of the rhino he'd seen at the watering hole. "Please, Mr. Crosby! Don't do it!"

There was a *dufff*, as something was flung at the door, and Hal and Winston jumped back, grabbing at each other.

"Let's go," Winston urged.

They heard an explosive *CRACK!*, followed by ear-ringing silence, then a heavy *THUD*.

CHAPTER TWELVE

SHOOTING
ON THE STAR

Was that a gunshot?" Hal looked at Winston, who was wide-eyed.

"Did he do it? Did he shoot the rhino?" Winston whispered.

"Mr. Crosby?" Hal called out, listening for an answer, but none came. He pressed his ear to the door. Over the rumble and squeak of the train's wheels, he could hear someone moving about inside the compartment.

"Mr. Crosby? Are you okay?" He looked at Winston. "I think we should go and wait in the observation car, like Uncle Nat said."

Winston nodded, and they hurried back up the corridor.

"Wait." Winston turned round.

"What is it?"

"Chipo! Where is she?"

"There!" Hal pointed. The mongoose was right at the other end of the corridor, standing in a thin slice of sunlight on the carpet. The yellow light was coming from the doorway to Portia and Patrice's compartment, which was ajar. Chipo glanced back at Winston, then disappeared through the gap.

"Uh-oh," said Winston, moving after her.

Hal grabbed his arm. "But we need to get to the observation car!"

"I have to get her—I'll be in big trouble if Chipo upsets any more passengers."

"Quickly, then!"

They hurried on tiptoe to the open door of the compartment.

"Why is it open?" Winston whispered, sliding it back a little further and peeping inside.

"Maybe they didn't shut the door properly when they left."

"Chipo!" Winston hissed. "Chipo, where are you?"

Hal grabbed Winston by the shoulder, pointing. Lying in the double bed at the far end of the room was Patrice Mbatha, his face covered by an eye mask. The boys froze, watching his chest rise and fall.

"He's asleep," Hal whispered.

"Didn't the gunshot wake him?"

"Maybe he's a deep sleeper."

Winston spotted Chipo under the bed and sank down onto all fours, crawling into the room, holding out a hand to try to tempt her out.

Hal crept in after him, staring at Patrice, searching his face for any sign he was waking. Then he saw something yellow sticking out of his ear.

"Winston," he whispered, "he's wearing earplugs!"

"Chipo, come here," said Winston quietly, "come here, girl. That's it." Chipo ran out from under the bed to the connecting door. She scratched at it, then looked back at Winston.

"No, you can't go through there. Come here, you silly girl," he muttered.

"Where does that door go?" Hal whispered.

"Mervyn Crosby's compartment," Winston replied.

Hal saw the hook above the handle was down, locked into its cradle.

Chipo scratched at the door again. Winston dropped to all fours and crawled past Patrice, scooped up Chipo, and jumped to his feet. The two boys ran out of the compartment, carefully sliding the door shut, then scrambled into the observation car, collapsing into a seat and breathing heavily.

"Chipo, what were you doing in there, you mischievous mongoose?" Winston scolded.

Out of the observation car window, Hal saw a high wall of golden rock. They were in a canyon. "Do you think he hit it? The rhino I mean?"

"I hope not, but . . ." Winston frowned, looking out of the windows. "I'm surprised there was a rhino out here. You don't see them wandering around. There are so few of them left." He got to his feet and walked to the veranda. "Mama will be furious that he fired a gun out the window. He could've hurt something . . . Wait!" He looked over his shoulder at Hal. "Look." He pointed.

"What?"

"Don't you see it? Up there."

"See what?"

"Rhino Rock! That idiot was shooting at Rhino Rock."

The boys laughed with relief. Hal marveled at how real the rock formation looked from a distance, just like Greg, the fireman, had said.

"Did you hear that thud, though?" Hal said, as they sat back down.

"I hope the kickback from the gun was so powerful that Mr. Crosby fell over."

"But he's an experienced hunter. Surely he knows how to handle a gun."

Hearing footsteps and banging in the corridor, they looked at each other, listening hard.

"Mr. Crosby, it's Luther Ackerman. I'd like to speak with you. Please open the door." There was another knock. "Mr. Crosby? I'm told you've been shooting from the train." He knocked again, more insistently this time. "Mr. Crosby, if you don't let me in, I'll have to open the door with my key." He paused to let the warning sink in. "Do you hear me, Mr. Crosby?" He knocked again, then they heard the jangle of keys.

"Why isn't he answering?" Winston whispered.

A cold sensation crept across Hal's chest.

They heard a strangled exclamation, then Mr. Ackerman cried out Uncle Nat's name. There was a muddle of urgent male voices.

Hal looked at Winston. "Something's wrong." He stood up.

"Your uncle said we should stay here."

"I just want to look down the corridor and see what's happening," he said, going to the door.

The corridor was empty, until Luther Ackerman stepped backward out of Mervyn Crosby's cabin, his hands to his face. He was muttering, "Oh no! Oh no!" over and over again.

"Get Ryo Sasaki," Hal heard his uncle say in a commanding voice.

Luther Ackerman turned to hurry away. "Mr. Lovejoy!" he exclaimed as Erik appeared at the far end of the corridor.

"Is everything okay? You look like you've seen a ghost."

"Thank goodness you're here. There's been a terrible accident." He grabbed Erik's arm and pulled him to the compartment doorway. Erik stood, staring down.

"Is he . . . ?" Erik said.

"I'm afraid so," Uncle Nat replied from inside the compartment. Then, seeing Mr. Ackerman was still standing there, he shouted, "*Get Ryo Sasaki!*"

"I'm here! What is it?" Mr. Sasaki came up the corridor carrying his doctor's bag. Erik and Luther moved out of his way. He looked through the doorway, took out a pair of blue surgical gloves, pulled them on with a snap, and stepped inside.

Hal was frozen to the spot. What was going on in Mr. Crosby's cabin? He felt sick with fear.

Portia Ramaboa entered the corridor. "What is this?" she asked.

Erik looked at Mr. Ackerman, whose mouth was opening and closing like a fish as he made unintelligible sounds. He stepped forward to prevent Portia from coming close enough to see into the compartment. "Ms. Ramaboa, please step back. I'm afraid there's been a terrible accident."

"An accident?"

"What's he talking about?" Winston whispered. He was standing at Hal's shoulder.

"Something's happened to Mr. Crosby."

"What would you like the guests to do, Mr. Ackerman?" Erik asked the train manager.

"Hm? Errr, mmm, ah, um . . . ," Ackerman jabbered, looking about in panic. Hal felt fear crackle around his heart. He'd never seen grown-ups acting like this. Whatever had happened to Mr. Crosby, it must be very, very, bad.

"Mr. Ackerman would like all the guests to go to the lounge car, where he will be along shortly to explain the situation," Erik said with a cordial smile.

"Yes, yes, the lounge car. Good idea." Mr. Ackerman nodded, unable to stop himself from staring with horror into Mr. Crosby's compartment.

"What is going on?" Portia bent her neck, trying to see through the doorway.

"Ms. Ramaboa, please . . ." Erik stood firm.

"What's going on?" Patrice Mbatha appeared in his doorway, yawning and pulling out his earplugs. "Portia?" He took in the scene in the corridor. "Is everything all right?"

"Mr. Ackerman has requested that all guests go to the lounge car at once," Erik repeated. "Ms. Ramaboa, take Mr. Mbatha and inform any passengers you meet on the way. Mr. Ackerman will be there shortly."

Uncle Nat stepped out of Mr. Crosby's compartment.

"Is someone hurt?" asked Patrice, looking confused.

"We will go to the lounge." Portia nodded, taking Patrice's hand and leading him away.

"I must check on Hal," Uncle Nat said to Erik. "I don't think I can be of any more help here. Someone should find Mrs. Crosby and tell her what's happened."

Erik nodded, glancing at the distressed Luther Ackerman. "I'd better do it."

"Go! Go! Go!" Hal whispered frantically, and he and Winston scrambled back into their seats as Uncle Nat appeared in the doorway.

"What's going on?" Hal asked immediately. "What's happened to Mr. Crosby?"

Uncle Nat's expression was grave. "Mr. Crosby's had an accident."

"What kind of accident?" Winston asked.

"Is he hurt?" Hal asked, scanning his uncle's face and realizing with a chill that the truth was worse.

"Is he . . . dead?" Winston whispered, cuddling Chipo.

"I need you both to come with me to the lounge."

"Did he have a heart attack?" Hal asked, thinking of the loud thump they'd heard after the gun was fired.

"I can't answer any questions right now, Hal, so please don't ask me."

Uncle Nat shepherded them into the corridor. When he saw them, Mr. Ackerman stepped back into Mr. Crosby's compartment and shut the door.

CHAPTER THIRTEEN

AMELIA'S ACCUSATION

When Hal, Winston, and Uncle Nat arrived in the lounge, Portia and Patrice were sitting in a corner, speaking in hushed tones. Satsuki Sasaki was reading a book beside the bookshelf, and Beryl was at the bar ordering a drink. Uncle Nat sat them at the table by the board games and awkwardly suggested they play one, but neither boy was in the mood. Winston petted Chipo, while Hal opened his sketchbook and began to draw.

"Well, this is all very mysterious," Beryl said, joining them without being invited. "Why are we all being told to gather in the lounge?"

"There's been an accident," Uncle Nat replied in a low voice. "Mr. Crosby is hurt."

Beryl's eyebrows shot up, but she said nothing, taking a sip of her drink.

"Winston!" Liana cried out in relief as she rushed into the lounge. Uncle Nat moved so she could sit down beside Winston. She wrapped her arms around him in a bear hug. "You're safe."

"I'm fine, Mama. Oww, you're crushing me."

"Have you seen Erik?" Beryl asked.

Liana nodded. "He's in the dining car with Mrs. Crosby and her daughter."

Poor Nicole! Hal thought, realizing he'd been so consumed with curiosity that he'd forgotten his friend. Winston looked at him, obviously thinking the same thing.

Liana, Uncle Nat, and Beryl undertook a forced conversation about the wildlife they'd seen that day, in a transparent bid to reassure Hal and Winston, but their awkward exchanges made Hal even more alarmed.

Everyone stopped talking to watch Luther Ackerman hurry through the carriage. Five minutes later, he passed back through with two crew members. They resumed their stiff conversation until Ryo Sasaki entered. He went to sit with his wife, and Hal watched the pair have a hushed conversation in Japanese. Satsuki's eyes grew wide as her husband explained what was going on. She covered her mouth with her hand, trying not to cry, and Hal knew that the worst had happened.

Half an hour more ticked by before Erik Lovejoy came into the lounge car, accompanied by a fretful Luther Ackerman. An expectant hush fell over the carriage.

"Ladies and gentlemen, thank you for your patience," Erik said. "You may or may not know that up until five days ago, before I took early retirement, I was a detective with the Johannesburg Metropolitan Police Department. It is for this reason that Mr. Ackerman has asked me to take charge of this situation."

Mr. Ackerman nodded, wringing his hands.

"What situation?" Beryl asked.

"I am sorry to have to tell you that there has been an accident. One of your fellow passengers, Mr. Mervyn Crosby, is dead."

There was a shocked silence.

"An accident?" Patrice asked.

"It would seem that Mr. Crosby was attempting to shoot an animal from the window of his compartment when a mishap occurred and, well, he appears to have accidentally shot himself."

A murmur rippled around the room. Mr. Ackerman's hand-wringing intensified.

"How could he shoot himself?" Hal whispered.

"Maybe his gun malfunctioned," Winston replied. "Or the bullet exploded in the barrel."

"How ghastly," said Beryl with some relish.

"In a few hours we will reach the border town of Musina." Erik raised his voice to quiet the carriage. "We have already called ahead. There, Mr. Crosby will be taken off the train and, hopefully, the police will confirm our assessment of the situation."

"Those of you who wish to cut short your journey because of this tragedy may leave the train at Musina," said Mr. Ackerman. He looked ill. "But I hope you will stay for the second safari and to see the wonder of Victoria Falls!" His forced enthusiasm seemed hollow and distasteful.

"If anyone leaves this train," an angry voice called out, "they will be suspected of murder."

Everybody turned. Amelia Crosby stood in the doorway wearing a stony expression. Nicole was beside her, her face streaked with tears.

"Mrs. Crosby . . . ," Erik said in a soothing voice.

"No!" She glared at him. "Why won't you listen to me? I've told you. It's impossible for Merv to have shot himself."

"It's a terrible tragedy," said Mr. Ackerman, nodding madly.

"Merv's hunting rifle is the best money can buy," she insisted. "You told me that the gun is still intact, so it didn't malfunction, and the barrel is too long for him to have turned it on himself. He wouldn't have been able to reach the trigger." She folded her arms. "If he was shot, then somebody shot him." She looked around the room accusingly.

"I realize this is distressing, Mrs. Crosby," Erik said, in a calm and measured voice, "but the compartment was locked from the

111

inside. When Mr. Ackerman entered, the room was empty."

"What about the connecting door?" Mrs. Crosby glanced at Portia and Patrice.

"The connecting door was bolted—on both sides."

"You said the window was open."

"The train was in motion. No one could have climbed in or out." Erik looked at her sympathetically. "It is not just my assessment of the situation, Mrs. Crosby. Ryo Sasaki is a surgeon with extensive medical experience. He has examined your husband and agrees with my findings."

"I am so sorry for your loss." Ryo bowed his head. "His injuries are consistent with a wound caused by a bullet from the gun that he owned. I suspect that he opened the window, rested the gun on the frame, was about to pull the trigger when the rocking motion of the train unbalanced him, and he dropped it as it fired. It was . . . a very unfortunate accident."

"The rocking motion of the train unbalanced him?" Amelia Crosby scoffed. "He's been hunting all his life."

"Mom . . ." Nicole put a hand on her arm, but Amelia shook it off. She was furious. "No, *Mr.* Lovejoy, my husband was murdered, and by someone in this room." She stabbed her perfectly manicured fingernail in the air. "One of *you* shot him!"

"That's ridiculous," Patrice said, shaking his head.

"Is it?" Amelia looked at him, raising a well-groomed eyebrow. "You all hated him. Don't think that I don't know what you've all been saying about him, and me."

There was an uncomfortable silence, and Hal noticed everyone had looked down, embarrassed by the truth.

"This is murder, and you"—she turned back to Erik Lovejoy—"you are a detective from the Johannesburg police department . . ."

"A retired detective."

"You retired five days ago, yes?" she snapped.

He nodded.

"I bet, when you left, you had a heap of holiday time you hadn't taken."

Erik looked surprised but nodded.

"So, if you're on holiday, that means you haven't properly retired yet. Legally, you must still be a detective, and if you don't immediately start investigating the murder of my husband, I'm going to sue the Johannesburg police department for negligence." She turned to leave. "I'm sure I don't need to remind you, *Detective* Lovejoy, that I can afford the very best lawyers *and* we own the biggest media company in the world." She put her hand on Nicole's shoulder. "You'd better do a good job, or I'll destroy your reputation and that of every single police officer you've ever worked with."

With that, the two of them left.

For a long moment everyone stared at Erik. Then Beryl shivered with excitement, proclaiming, "A killer walks among us!"

CHAPTER FOURTEEN

THE MYSTERY
AT MUSINA

A killer does *not* walk among us," Erik snapped at Beryl.
Amelia's threat had clearly annoyed him.

"We can all sympathize with Mrs. Crosby. It's a shock when a loved one dies. I myself lost my brother recently, and there are some days when I can't believe he's gone." He cleared his throat. "However, she's right about my employment contract." He gave a tiny shake of his head and looked around the room. "For the sake of my department, I will have to undertake an investigation, at least until we get to Musina, where the local police can take over. But let me reassure you all: Mr. Ackerman, Mr. Sasaki, and I are certain this was an accident. There is no evidence to suggest that it wasn't."

"Can I ask . . ." Luther Ackerman leaned forward. "What will happen at the border, in Musina, if the South African police suspect a crime has taken place?"

"The train will be impounded, and we'll all be taken in for questioning."

"The journey will be cut short?" he exclaimed in dismay.

114

"Of course." Erik nodded.

"That'd be annoying," Beryl muttered. "Although . . . vital, I'm sure, for justice," she added quickly.

"And what if the police agree that it was an accident?" Patrice asked.

"Then Mrs. Crosby will have to accept their verdict. I presume she and her daughter would leave the train with Mr. Crosby, and we'd continue on our way."

Hal glanced around the group of passengers. It was obvious that all of them hoped Mervyn Crosby's death was an accident.

"Now, I must ask you all to return to your compartments and stay there until we've arrived in Musina and the police have finished their business," Erik said. "Mr. Ackerman has arranged for dinner to be served to you in your rooms. If I need to speak to you, I'll come and knock on your door."

***

The Safari Star rumbled across the plains toward Musina, its windows moving squares of gold in the blue dark of early evening. Inside their compartment, Hal sat opposite his uncle at the table, looking down at a delicious dinner of *boerewors* (a long coiled barbecued sausage) and *chakalaka* (a salad of onions, tomatoes, peppers, carrots, beans, and spices). Despite it being a long time since high tea, he had little appetite, because he couldn't stop thinking about Mervyn Crosby. He noticed Uncle Nat wasn't eating, either.

"What are you thinking about?" he asked.

"Oh, nothing much." Uncle Nat pushed some food onto his fork but didn't bring it to his mouth.

115

"Erik said that he, Mr. Sasaki, and Mr. Ackerman thought Mr. Crosby's death was an accident, but you were inside that room too." He left his comment hanging in the air.

Uncle Nat nodded, and Hal could see he was struggling with something.

"Why don't you want to tell me?"

"It's not that I don't *want* to tell you. It's more that, to be a responsible grown-up, I *shouldn't* tell you. You're very young—"

"I'm twelve!"

"You've had a very distressing day, what with that snake, and now this, and, well, we came out here for you to draw animals . . ." He put his hands under his glasses and rubbed his eyes. "I suspect I'm the worst uncle in existence."

"You think Mr. Crosby was murdered, don't you?" Hal put down his knife and fork.

"I honestly don't know, Hal. But if I were Amelia Crosby, I'd be demanding an investigation, too. I can't believe that Mervyn Crosby would accidentally shoot himself, and . . ." He sighed. "You were right. Luther Ackerman is behaving very oddly."

"You don't think . . ." Hal grabbed his sketchbook, opening it to the picture of Ackerman being given a roll of money. He looked up at his uncle. "You don't think Mr. Ackerman was paid to murder Mr. Crosby?"

"No! Why would he do that? You mustn't jump to conclusions. After all, practically every passenger on this train has a reason to want Mervyn Crosby out of the way. He wasn't a very nice man."

"So we *are* investigating?" Hal tried not to look too eager.

"Oh dear. Look, I agree that something's not quite right here . . ."

"So why shouldn't we try and solve the case?"

"Because this could be *murder*, Hal!" Uncle Nat drummed his fingers on the table. "If Amelia is right, and her husband *was* killed, then this is a very dangerous train for us to be on."

"So I shouldn't tell you what I heard when the gun was fired?"

"What do you mean?"

"I was standing outside his compartment door when the gun went off."

"But I told you go to the observation car."

"And we *were* going," Hal said, "but I . . . may have banged on the door and begged Mr. Crosby not to shoot the rhino one last time." He paused, a horrible thought occurring to him. "Oh no! What if I made him trip and drop the gun?"

117

"I don't think that's very likely. He knew you were there." Uncle Nat waved that idea away. "What did you hear?"

"I heard Mr. Crosby slide the window open. It made a click as it hit the bottom of the frame. I shouted, and he threw something at the door, something soft."

"It was a cushion." Uncle Nat nodded. "It was on the floor when I went in."

"Then we heard the shot and a heavy thud."

"All of that corroborates Erik's theory that it was an accident."

"Yes, but I called out, asking if he was okay. I put my ear to the door and *I heard someone moving about*, from one side of the room to the other."

"You're sure?"

Hal nodded. "How could Mr. Crosby have been moving around if he'd just been shot?"

"He couldn't have. His body was on the floor beside the tipped-over chair. He landed where he fell and didn't get up again." He paused. "But that points the finger at Patrice Mbatha, in the compartment next door."

Hal shook his head. "He slept through the whole thing. Winston and I went into his compartment right after—"

"You did *what*?"

"Chipo was scared by the gunshot. She ran into his compartment. We had to go in after her. Patrice was fast asleep wearing earplugs with an eye mask on. He didn't see us sneak in and grab her."

"I don't know why I'm surprised." Uncle Nat looked incredulous. "But you're right, it can't have been Patrice. The Crosbys' compartment was locked from the inside. I checked the connecting door." He frowned. "But who did you hear? And where did they go?"

Hal looked down at his sketchbook. "If this is a murder, then we have to solve it."

Uncle Nat closed his eyes. "Your mother is going to kill me."

As they talked, they ate, and without noticing, they cleaned their plates. Pudding was a *melktert*, which Hal was pleased to discover was pastry filled with custard. He polished off his and then Uncle Nat's.

"Are we at Musina?" Hal asked as the train pulled into a siding. White police cars with blue flashing lights were waiting on a dirt road beside the track. He pressed his face to the glass and saw figures in white plastic suits emerging from a van. "They've brought a forensics team." He looked at his uncle. "Do you think they'll let me watch them work?"

"No, and neither will I! Forensics is not a spectator sport. Anyway, Erik asked that we stay in our compartments while the police do their work."

There was a knock, and Winston stuck his head round the door. "Hello, Mr. Bradshaw. I was wondering if Hal wanted to come to Chipo's compartment to work on the mongoose run with me?"

"I'd love to," said Hal, getting up from the table. "If that's okay?"

"Stay out of Erik's way," Uncle Nat said with a nod, and the boys disappeared out the door.

They ran down the train to the service car. Hal slowed as they approached Winston and Chipo's compartment, but Winston kept walking. "Where are you going?"

"To watch the police. Come on."

"What if we get caught?"

"We won't," Winston said, opening the carriage door and clambering down the ladder on the far side of the train. "I thought you were a detective?"

Chipo jumped down onto his shoulder, then to the ground, darting about in the long grass beside the train, trying to catch a large moth. "Come on," Winston hissed. "If anyone catches us, we'll say Chipo needed a wee."

Hal followed him down the ladder. The door swung shut with a *clunk*. They both froze, looking around to see if anyone had heard them, but nothing happened.

"This way." Winston marched off, keeping close to the carriages. "The police are on the other side."

On their right, shadowy warehouses were fenced off by a chain-link fence. As they neared the rear of the train, blue light from the police cars flashed through the bogies under the carriages. Hal saw a familiar silhouette walk past Mr. Crosby's window, and he grabbed Winston. Putting his finger to his lips, he dragged Winston down to squat in the shadow of the wheels.

"It's Erik," Hal whispered, pointing up.

"Of course not," Erik was saying. "We proceed as planned."

They heard the murmur of a woman's voice, but it was too quiet to make out what she was saying.

"Exactly. We both know what's at stake here." Erik nodded. "I feel for the wife, but she's refusing to accept the facts."

The woman replied, but Hal only caught the word *accident*.

"The man was a clumsy oaf. It's poetic justice that he shot himself while trying to kill a rhino."

The woman said something else unintelligible.

"We both know that there are more important matters at stake here. Take the samples, fingerprint the place, photograph, do everything your team needs to wrap this mess up, but be quick. We have a schedule to keep. When I think of the time and energy we've put into this operation . . ." He shook his head.

The woman spoke again. Hal strained to listen, but it was no use.

"I'm glad you agree. We can't have it all fall to pieces now. I won't let some silly accident mess up years of hard work. It's vital that the Safari Star continues its journey."

CHAPTER FIFTEEN

THE RECONSTRUCTION

The boys ran back to the service car, Winston clutching Chipo in his arms. "Mr. Lovejoy told us he was retired," he said breathlessly, as they clambered aboard the train.

"That didn't sound retired to me," Hal said. "He's investigating a case, and Mr. Crosby's murder is threatening to ruin it."

"You think he was definitely murdered, then?" Winston said, shutting the carriage door.

"I don't know. Erik seems certain it was an accident, but Uncle Nat's not so sure. If Erik doesn't want a murder investigation to interfere with his other case, maybe he's only seeing what he wants to see. We should go and tell Uncle Nat what we heard."

***

When he opened the door to their compartment, Hal found Uncle Nat lying on the carpet in an awkward position, staring up at the ceiling.

"Oh!" Uncle Nat sprang to his feet. "Hello, you're back quickly."

Hal eyed the chair lying on its side beneath the window, which was wide open. "What are you doing?"

"Nothing."

"Are you reconstructing the scene of the crime?"

"Shh!" Uncle Nat hurried over and slid the door shut. "Okay, yes, that's what I'm doing."

"Brilliant!" said Winston. "Can we help?"

"Only if you're quiet," said Uncle Nat.

"We found out something important." Hal lowered his voice. "Erik Lovejoy isn't retired. He's undercover, working a big case."

"How on earth did you discover that?"

"We overheard him talking to a police officer. He's worried that Mr. Crosby's death could jeopardize their case."

"You learned this in your compartment, did you?" Uncle Nat frowned at Winston.

"Er, Chipo needed a wee," Winston said quickly. "We took her outside, to go by the wheels of the train."

"And she just happened to wee by the wheels of Mr. Crosby's compartment?" Uncle Nat chuckled as both boys nodded. "Well, I'm beginning to think that Erik is right about it being an accident. Our compartment isn't as big as Mr. Crosby's, but it's essentially the same layout—without the Jacuzzi bath and king-sized bed . . ."

"The Royal Suite has a Jacuzzi bath?" Hal was impressed.

"It is the *Royal* Suite," Winston pointed out.

"If there was a killer in Mr. Crosby's compartment, where did they vanish to?" Uncle Nat threw his hands up. "There's no way in or out."

"Is everything exactly where it was when you found him?"

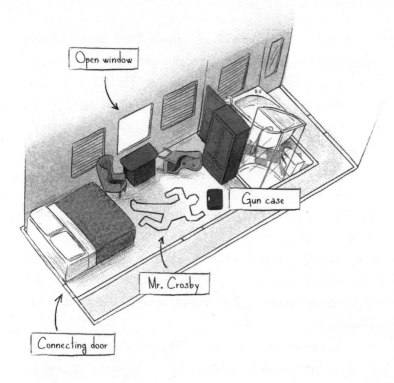

Open window

Gun case

Mr. Crosby

Connecting door

Hal asked, sitting down at the table and opening his sketchbook.

"Yes. Let's walk it through. I'm Mr. Crosby." Uncle Nat stepped out into the hall, then opened the door and walked in. "I'm excited to shoot the rhino."

"Which was actually Rhino Rock," Winston chipped in.

"I don't want you troublesome children to ruin things, so . . ." He locked the door. "Then I take down my gun case from the luggage rack above the bed."

"How big is the case?" Hal asked.

"About the size of a saxophone case. I put it on the floor here." He mimed opening it and taking out a gun as Hal drew it into his diagram of the carriage. "I load the gun with bullets from the box in the case. I go over to the window and immediately see that the height isn't good and the rocking train will make it hard to keep a steady aim, so I pull the chair over." He righted the chair and put it in position. "Nathaniel Bradshaw is banging on the door threatening to get Luther Ackerman, so I tell him to go do it. Then I sit down, laying the gun across my lap, and slide the window open." Uncle Nat mimed opening the window.

"I hear you doing it, and I bang on the door, begging you not to shoot the rhino," Hal continued, marking the open window on his diagram.

"I take the cushion from the back of the chair and hurl it at the door to shut you up," Uncle Nat said. "Then I lift the gun and rest my elbows on the window casing. I lean forward and take aim."

"We hear a shot, then a thud," Winston said.

"It could have happened like this"—Uncle Nat mimed his elbow slipping from the window frame—"causing me to let go the butt of the gun. It falls to the ground, barrel spinning up. *Bang!* The gun goes off as the butt hits the ground, shooting me." He tipped the chair backward so it fell onto the carpet with a thud, then rolled out of it so that he was spread-eagled on the floor. "This is the exact position he was found in."

Hal drew the outline of a figure on the floor.

"It works." Uncle Nat sat up. "The accidental shooting is a very strong theory."

"Except I heard someone moving around after the shot," Hal pointed out.

"Maybe someone was in there with him when the accident happened?" Winston suggested.

"So then why didn't they raise the alarm and open the door?" Uncle Nat asked. "And where were they when Luther and I came in?"

"We've walked through the accident scenario. Let's try it with a murderer," Hal suggested.

"I'll be the murderer," Winston volunteered. "Would I be in here already? Waiting for Mr. Crosby?"

"Yes, there's no way into the compartment once I lock the door." Uncle Nat mimed entering the cabin and taking down the gun case. "But where are you hiding? And you have to shoot him with his own gun. If you spring out and take my gun from me, there'd be a struggle, and you boys would have heard."

"What if I'm not in the compartment but come in through the window when you open it?" Winston went to the open casement and looked out into the still night. Steadying himself against the frame, he stepped onto the sill, reached up to the roof, and pulled himself out.

Hal looked out. Winston's face appeared over the edge of the roof, grinning in the moonlight. "I grabbed the mushroom vent," he said. "It was pretty easy."

"Because the train's not moving," Hal pointed out. "It'd be much harder if we were traveling at speed. Try to get in from up there."

Uncle Nat repositioned the chair and sat down as Winston rearranged himself on the roof.

"Go!" Hal called up, and Winston's legs dangled into view. They kicked around searching for the edge of the window, then he lowered himself, immediately treading on Uncle Nat, who pretended to cry out and tumbled back in the chair.

"It doesn't work," Hal said. "Mr. Crosby would have yelled and shot at the intruder."

"What if . . ." Winston paused to think. "If . . . the murderer was waiting on the roof? Then, when Mr. Crosby points his gun out the window, he grabs the gun from him, shoots Crosby, drops the gun into the compartment, and then goes back to lying on the roof while all the commotion takes place?"

"That could work, if he were Spider-Man," Hal said.

"Not many people on this train could climb through that window, or grab a gun from the roof while the train was moving," Uncle Nat pointed out. "It would be very dangerous. Patrice is strong enough, but he's too broad to climb through the window."

"And we saw him asleep on the other side of the locked door," Hal said.

"What about the crew?" Uncle Nat looked at Winston.

"Mama could probably do it," Winston said. "She's experienced at handling guns, but she wouldn't." He shook his head. "Even though the people working on this train didn't like Mr. Crosby, they wouldn't risk spending their life in prison to kill him."

"Let's rule out the window as an entry or an exit point for now," Uncle Nat said. "What about if someone had been lying in wait for Mr. Crosby?"

"They could have hidden in the bathroom," suggested Hal, "or in the wardrobe?"

Uncle Nat opened the wardrobe, swept the hangers to one side, and got in, closing the door behind him. "A bit of a squeeze," came his muffled voice, and Hal and Winston laughed as the door swung open. "But Erik would have found the murderer when he searched the room, and Ryo or I would've seen them."

"Could someone have crept out the main door and run away while Winston and I were in Patrice's compartment?"

BEFORE

Fishing wire

"They'd have to be very fast and quiet," Winston pointed out. "And lock the door behind them."

"Amelia Crosby has a key," Uncle Nat said.

"The killer could have taken Mr. Crosby's key from him," said Hal, thinking it through. "But where would they have gone after leaving the compartment? They didn't go into the observation car. It was empty."

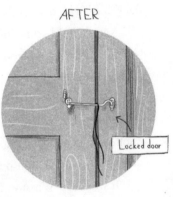

AFTER

Locked door

"I ran to the lounge to get Luther, and the two of us came straight back," Uncle Nat said, his brow furrowing. "I didn't see anyone."

"My head's spinning." Winston dropped into the armchair. "Someone *must* have been in the compartment, because Hal heard them."

"What about the other way out?" Hal said, going to the connecting door into Beryl's compartment. He peered at the lock. It was a brass hook on a hinge that dropped into a slot on the wall to prevent the door being pulled open.

"There's a lock on each side," said Uncle Nat. "Both have to be undone for the door to open. But both of them were locked."

"Does anyone have any string?" asked Hal.

Winston rummaged in his pockets, producing a tangle of fishing wire, along with some dried fruit and a compass.

"You're going to fish for answers?" he asked.

"I want to test something," said Hal, fastening the fishing wire to the top of the hook. "Uncle Nat, could you ask Beryl if she'd open the door for us on her side?" A minute later he heard Uncle Nat's low voice through the door.

"Of course, darling," Beryl squealed. "I love a spot of amateur sleuthing." The door slid open. "Hello, boys."

"Is it okay if I come in?" Hal asked.

"Certainly." Beryl stood back, looking curious.

Hal lifted the hook on their side of the door to the up position, looped the wire round it, and stepped into Beryl's room. "Let me back in if this works," he said to Winston as he slid the door shut. Gently pulling at the fishing wire, he heard the hook on the other side fall into the slot with a *click*.

"It worked!" Winston called out, opening the door.

"What did?" Beryl asked excitedly.

"We've just proved it's possible to lock a connecting door from the other side," Hal said, dropping to his knees to draw the lock trick.

"That's thrilling!" Beryl clapped her hands together.

Winston opened the door. "Hal, do you think the killer could have exited Mr. Crosby's compartment, locked the door behind him, and hidden in Patrice's room while he was sleeping?"

Hal nodded. "It's possible."

"But that would mean we were in the room with the murderer!"

CHAPTER SIXTEEN

DEPUTY DETECTIVES

Hal? Wake up. The border police are here."

Hal sat up and rubbed his eyes. "Are we continuing on to Zimbabwe?"

Uncle Nat was dressed in white chinos and a dark blue blazer and stood at the window, sipping a glass of water. "It looks like it, once they've checked our passports and visas. You'd better get dressed."

Hal got up and splashed water on his face.

"So the police agreed with Erik?" he asked, wriggling into his clothes. "They think Mr. Crosby's death was accidental?"

"It seems so. We've had a note under our door—Erik has asked everyone to meet in the dining car once the inspections are complete."

An officer in a gray-blue shirt appeared at their door. Hal's heart pounded unnecessarily as she examined their visas, but the officer smiled and nodded. "Welcome to Zimbabwe," she said, returning their passports before moving on down the train.

"Right," said Uncle Nat. "Breakfast. Time to hear what Erik has to say."

The mood in the dining car was tense. Beryl waved at them. "I've saved you seats!"

Winston was sitting beside his mother at the next table. Hal whispered hello to him as he slid into his seat. He took out his tin of charcoal and set to work sketching Portia and Patrice, who were at their usual table in the corner. Patrice was sullen, and Portia's expression was calm, but she was twisting and twisting her napkin. Ryo and Satsuki must have been up early, because they had food in front of them. Hal paused as Nicole came in with her mother. They ignored everyone in the room as they took their table. Hal decided to go and talk to Nicole, to see if he could help, as soon as he had the chance.

Erik Lovejoy entered, moving to the middle of the room so everyone could see and hear him. "Thank you all for being here," he said. "As you know, yesterday evening the police completed a full inspection of Mr. Crosby's compartment. They came to the conclusion that his death was a tragic accident. His body has been removed from the train, and his compartment will remain locked and out of bounds."

Hal glanced at Amelia Crosby, wondering if the news would upset her, but her expression was as unreadable as stone.

"This means we can complete our journey," Luther Ackerman interrupted, exhibiting an insensitive amount of delight. "The border police have completed their checks, too, so we're off to Zimbabwe! If we leave now, we should still reach the Hwange National Park in time for our second safari this afternoon." He looked around the room, beaming. But, seeing the passengers' incredulous expressions, he cleared his throat, and blushed.

Erik looked at Mr. Ackerman with distaste. "The authorities believe Mr. Crosby's death to have been an accident," he continued. "However, Mrs. Crosby is not satisfied with their conclusion. After a long discussion with her last night, I have agreed to work on her behalf, to look into the events that led to the shooting."

A thin smile crept across Amelia's face.

"As I have no jurisdiction in Zimbabwe, I will be acting as a private investigator. I will do everything in my power to eliminate every possibility of foul play."

There was a murmur at this news, and Hal felt a thrill of excitement.

"I appreciate that having a private investigator on board while you enjoy your holiday is not what you signed up for when you bought your ticket for the Safari Star, so I would like anyone who has any objections to raise them now."

"I think we would all feel more able to relax if we knew for certain what happened to Mr. Crosby," Portia said.

"I think it's wonderfully generous of you," piped up Beryl, fluttering her eyelashes at Erik. "And anyone who doesn't want yesterday's tragic incident investigated immediately casts suspicion upon themselves." She peered round at the other passengers.

"I'm more than happy for you to investigate," announced Patrice, thumping the table so that the crockery rattled. "The more thorough you are, the quicker we can move on."

There were murmurs of agreement.

Amelia Crosby got to her feet. "I'm grateful for your cooperation," she said. "My daughter and I are staying aboard the Safari Star to ensure Detective Lovejoy has the support he needs." Hal wondered whether she had offered Erik a lot of money, or if she was just very good at twisting arms. "And if one of you killed my husband, I will make sure you rot in jail for the rest of your life." She sat back down abruptly.

"Full steam ahead!" Luther pronounced to a roomful of glares.

"Thank you for your understanding." Erik bowed his head. "I would like to get started as soon as possible. After breakfast, I will interview each of you to establish a clear timeline of yesterday's events. But for now, please, eat."

The room was soon filled with the scraping of cutlery and the rasp of knives on toast.

Beryl leaned out to grab Erik's hand. "You were amazing. What a brilliant idea to become a private detective and solve the case!"

"It wasn't my idea," Erik replied, allowing Beryl to pull him down to sit next to her. He looked at Uncle Nat and lowered his voice. "I still think it was an accident, but if it makes Mrs. Crosby happy and means the train can complete its journey, where's the harm? I'm going to be swift and methodical, so as not to ruin everyone's holiday." He poured himself a coffee.

"I've pursued some lines of inquiry myself," Hal said, hoping he sounded professional.

"More drawings?" Erik asked.

Hal nodded, opening his sketchbook. "I've mapped out the crime scene, and yesterday evening we staged a reconstruction to test out a number of possible theories . . ."

"Really?" Erik smiled, glancing at Uncle Nat. "You know, ordinarily, I would conduct an investigation with a deputy—someone to bounce theories off of and help organize the case." He paused. "I've heard about the previous cases you've solved in Scotland and

America. I was wondering . . . Would you like to be my deputy, Harrison?"

Hal was surprised and delighted by the question. His mouth fell open. "I . . . I . . . well, yes, please, I mean. Thank you."

"Can I be one, too?" Winston had turned round in his seat and was listening.

"Winston, how fortuitous," Erik said in a serious voice. "I was about to ask you if you wanted to join the team."

"Really?" Winston looked pleased.

"If it's okay with your mother." Erik looked at Liana, and she nodded.

"Winston needs something useful to keep him occupied. He and Chipo are driving the kitchen staff mad."

"Do everything Detective Lovejoy asks, Hal." Uncle Nat gave him a look laced with meaning. "You might *learn* something."

"I doubt that there's a murderer to catch, but he'll certainly learn how to make a strong cup of coffee," Erik said, and everyone laughed.

Hal nodded at his uncle, knowing he was alluding to the secret case they'd overheard Erik talking about the previous night.

CHAPTER SEVENTEEN

CROCODILE TEARS

As they ate their breakfast there was a blast of steam, and the Safari Star pulled her carriages out of the siding at Musina. From the window of the dining car, Hal watched the train roll onto the Alfred Beit Bridge high above the snaking Limpopo River, its currents churning up the silt to make the water brown. The river marked the border of South Africa and their entry into Zimbabwe. Hal felt a shiver of pleasure at the thought of entering a new country.

"The Limpopo is famous for its man-eating crocodiles," said Beryl.

Hal looked at her skeptically.

"It's true! I heard a wonderfully gruesome story about a smuggler who fed his enemies to them." She blinked. "Actually, that's rather good, isn't it?" She pulled her journal from her handbag and scribbled it down, leaving Hal uncertain as to whether she'd made it up.

After breakfast, Detective Lovejoy invited Hal and Winston to a compartment Mr. Ackerman had made available for him to work from. It was an empty deluxe suite, like Hal and Nat's, but the armchairs had been moved aside for a table and chairs from the dining car.

"You should get a sign for the door saying PRIVATE DETECTIVE," Winston suggested.

"I think that might be a bit much." Erik laughed.

"What do you want us to do?" Hal asked eagerly.

"I'm going to invite our suspects to be interviewed one by one and take their statements about the events that took place yesterday evening. I'll ask each guest to tell me their movements after high tea, and to tell me about their relationship with Mr. Crosby. I'd like you to make notes of everything you hear. If you have a question you want to ask, then you can—but you mustn't give away what other people have said. Do you understand?"

Hal swallowed. He'd never interviewed suspects officially before and felt nervous. He wanted to do a good job. "I could draw a plan of the train and mark where each person was at the time of the murder."

Erik nodded. "Great idea."

"I'll need a bigger sheet of paper." Hal opened the bedside drawer and took out a sheet of letter size paper watermarked with the Safari Star's logo.

"Now, before everyone else, I should interview you two. Nathaniel tells me you were together, outside Mr. Crosby's door, and heard the shot from his gun."

"Yes," said Hal with a nod, and then he and Winston took turns explaining what had happened before and after the gunshot.

"You say Mr. Mbatha's compartment door was ajar?" asked Erik, making a note. "But that he was inside, fast asleep?"

"Yes," answered Winston. "That's how Chipo got into the room."

Hal frowned. Listening to Winston describe it, the fact that Patrice's door had been ajar now struck him as odd.

"Well, I think that covers everything," said Erik, examining his notes. "Unless the two of you have anything you'd like to tell me?"

"Only that I'm certain I heard someone moving around the compartment *after* the shooting took place," Hal said.

"I've noted that already." Erik nodded. "Very strange."

Winston looked at Erik's list of passengers. "Who do we talk to first?"

"Let's start with Amelia Crosby," Erik replied with a dry smile. "I'll ask Khaya to bring her."

Five minutes later, a blank-looking Amelia Crosby glided into the compartment and sank into the empty armchair set out for her. She looked at Hal and Winston, who were sitting side by side at the table, then at Erik, who seated himself opposite her. "What are the children doing here?"

"Do you remember a few months back, the billionaire August Reza's daughter was kidnapped in America?"

Amelia Cooper Crosby

"Of course I remember," she said sniffily. "I've met August many times at social functions."

"Then you'll remember the case was solved by a boy." He pointed at Hal, who immediately blushed. "That boy was Harrison Beck."

Amelia examined Hal as if seeing him for the first time. "If

138

I remember rightly, the police wouldn't listen to you, but you investigated anyway and solved the case on your own?"

"That's correct," Erik said, before Hal could reply. "I thought a unique perspective on this matter was a good idea."

"It *is* a good idea, because, like I told you, Merv would never have had an accident with a gun. He could take one apart in his sleep. Somebody killed him and made it look like an accident: I *know* it, and it scares me." She leaned forward and whispered. "What if they want Nicole or me out of the way, too?"

It hadn't occurred to Hal that Mrs. Crosby might be frightened. He studied her, seeing that her iron-straight hair was curling and one of her nails was broken. He stood up. "Please don't worry, Mrs. Crosby. I won't let anything happen to you or Nicole."

"I'd like to echo what Harrison says. If it would make you feel safer, I'll ask Luther to station a member of the crew outside your door," Erik said.

"It would, thank you." Amelia nodded.

"I need to ask you about your movements yesterday afternoon." Erik clicked his pen. "Where did you go when you left the observation car, after high tea?"

"I followed Nic back to her compartment, in the next carriage along from mine and Merv's. I'm sure you heard she had a row with her father."

"I wasn't present," Erik said. "What was the argument about?"

"Nic's really bright"—Amelia smiled proudly—"and she wants to go to Harvard to study business, but Merv wasn't keen on the idea. That Portia woman brought up the subject of Nic going to college when we were on safari, and it got his hackles up. At high tea he told Nic he didn't want her to go, and it ended how

139

it always ends, with Nic storming off and me running after her. We went into her compartment, and I calmed her down, reassuring her that she'd be able to go to college." She tilted her head. "There's a way of handling Merv, to get what you want. I ran Nic a bath and watched TV while she had a soak. I didn't want to go back and deal with Merv's temper. He's an awful hothead." She stopped herself. "He *was* an awful hothead . . ." Her voice petered out and she stared into space.

"How long did you watch television for?" Erik asked gently.

"Until someone came to say you wanted to see me and Nic in the dining car." She blinked, but Hal noticed that her eyes hadn't filled with tears.

"Did your husband have any enemies that you knew of, Mrs. Crosby?" Erik asked.

Hal was startled by Amelia's laugh. "Let's be straight, shall we? Everybody hates Merv, and he liked it that way. He thought it was a sign of his success."

"Do *you* hate him?" Erik asked. Hal held his breath.

"Not anymore." Amelia gave him a sour smile. "It wasn't easy being Mervyn Crosby's wife." She shook her head. "I'm sure you'll find this out, so I'm going to save you some time. *All* of his money goes to Nicole. I signed a prenup that means his death will provide me with little more than a modest house and an allowance." She leaned forward. "I may not have loved my husband, Mr. Lovejoy, but I damn well love my daughter, and if Merv was killed for his money, then she's in danger, and I'll do whatever it takes to protect her."

"As will I," Erik assured her. "Thank you for your candor, Mrs. Crosby."

She sat back. "Call me Amelia."

"Do you recognize anyone on this train as an enemy of your husband's?"

"No. None that I'd call a serious enemy or even business rival. That's what makes this so frightening."

"Thank you. That's all the questions I have for now. Would you mind if we spoke to your daughter next?"

She got up. "I'll send Nic in."

When the door closed, Hal and Winston looked at each other.

"Well, I never expected that!" Hal whispered.

"Remember," Erik said, "we listen and note down facts. She did a very good job of making us feel sorry for her, but Amelia Crosby is an intelligent woman. She knows what she's doing."

"I believe that she's frightened, though," Hal replied.

"Yes." Erik nodded. "So do I."

There was a quiet knock at the door, and Nicole shuffled in. When she saw Hal and Winston, she looked confused but relieved.

"Are you all right?" Hal asked, and she nodded.

Winston brought Chipo over, and she rubbed noses with Nicole, which made her smile.

Nicole Crosby

"We're Detective Lovejoy's deputies," Hal explained.

"We're helping," said Winston with a grin, and Nicole relaxed a little.

"Do I sit here?" She pointed at the chair.

"You can sit wherever you like," Erik said kindly. "I only have a couple of questions for you."

Nicole sat down, pulling her blond curls back from her face and making a bun with a scrunchie from her pocket. "Okay, what do you want to know?"

"Your mother says that after the row with your father she followed you back to your compartment and ran you a bath."

"Yes." Nicole nodded.

"Once you were in the bath, did you talk to your mother or get out for any reason?"

"No. I heard Mom switch on the TV, but we didn't talk."

"How long were you in the bath for?"

Nicole shrugged. "Forty-five minutes. Then Mom knocked on the door and said you wanted to see us in the dining car."

Erik nodded. "That's all I have for you, unless you know of some reason why anybody on this train might want to harm your father?"

Nicole let out a deep, soul-weary sigh. "My father was a cruel man." She paused. "People think he's bad, but they don't *really* know. I've seen him destroy people's lives. He kills animals for fun." She looked at Hal and Winston. "I used to be scared that I'd end up like him. But then someone taught me that nobody gets to choose what kind of person I'm going to be, except me." She looked defiant.

"That's good advice," said Erik. "Who gave it to you?"

"Portia Ramaboa. She's one of the mentors of the International Young Women in Business Forum. She's really inspiring."

"How long have you known her?"

"I met her for the first time on this train," Nicole said. "But

142

we've been writing to each other for a few months. She really gets me." She swallowed. "You all think I'm sad about my pop, but"— her bottom lip trembled—"I'm not. He was a terrible person. And then I think, what if not being sad makes me a bad person, too?" She let out a sob.

Winston hurried forward, pulling a packet of tissues from his shorts and offering one to her. "You are a good person, and I think you're very brave," he said. "And Chipo agrees, don't you, Chipo?"

At the sound of her name, Chipo let out a squeak, and Nicole's sob mixed with a laugh.

Erik looked at Hal and nodded at the door.

"That's all the questions we have," Hal said, coming over. "You can go now."

"Thanks." She gave him a bleary smile.

"Get some rest," Erik said as she left the compartment.

There was a long silence once she'd gone. Hal was taken aback at how complicated Nicole's feelings were, and he felt grateful for his ordinary, loving family.

"Well now, Detectives, did we find out anything useful in that interview?"

"Yes," Hal said, returning to his seat at the table. He looked down at the quick sketches he'd done of Amelia and Nicole as they were questioned and marked their locations on his diagram. "We learned that Nicole and Portia knew each other before the train left Pretoria. And, if Nicole was undisturbed in the bathtub for forty-five minutes . . . that means Amelia doesn't have an alibi for her husband's death."

"Bingo," said Erik Lovejoy.

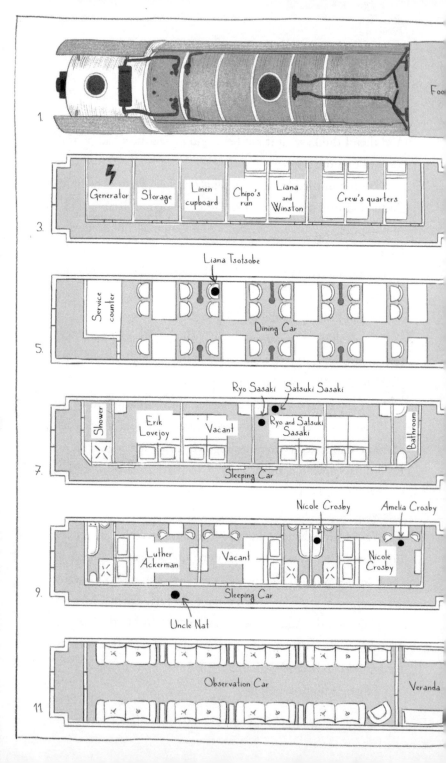

1.

3.
Generator | Storage | Linen cupboard | Chipo's run | Liana and Winston | Crew's quarters

Foo

5.
Liana Tsotsobe
Service counter
Dining Car

7.
Ryo Sasaki   Satsuki Sasaki
Shower | Erik Lovejoy | Vacant | Ryo and Satsuki Sasaki | Bathroom
Sleeping Car

9.
Nicole Crosby   Amelia Crosby
Luther Ackerman | Vacant | Nicole Crosby
Sleeping Car
Uncle Nat

11.
Observation Car   Veranda

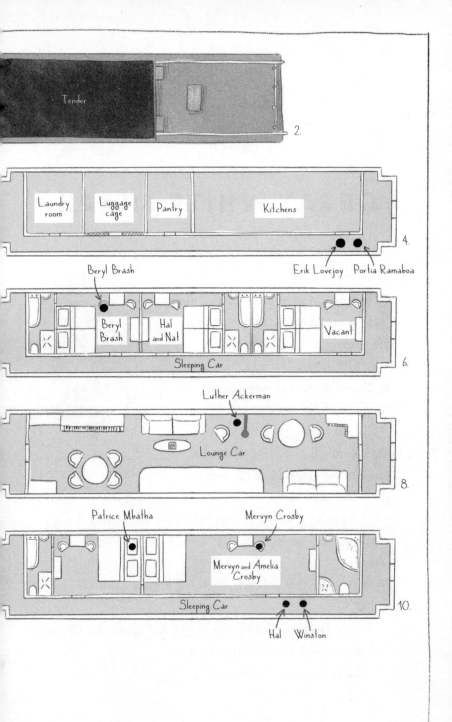

CHAPTER EIGHTEEN

GREAT WHITE SHARK

Patrice Mbatha

Patrice Mbatha prowled into the compartment, sitting at an angle and stretching out his legs. "Gentlemen," he said, bathing all three of them in a generous smile, "how can I be of service?"

"If you could, Mr. Mbatha, we'd like you to tell us what you did after you left the observation car yesterday afternoon," Erik said.

"I went back to my compartment for an afternoon nap." He held up his hands. "That's it. I was asleep at the time of the shooting."

"I thought only old people and babies took naps," Winston teased.

Patrice laughed. "It's beauty sleep." He patted his cheeks. "Keeps me looking fresh for the cameras."

"Didn't the gunshot wake you?"

"I wear earplugs and an eye mask, a habit I picked up from napping in my trailer on set. I heard nothing at all."

"What did wake you up?" Hal asked. "You came out of your compartment and asked, 'What's going on?'"

"I have a vibrating alarm on my watch." He held his wrist up. "I was planning to have a shower and get ready for dinner, but when I sat up in bed I saw people gathered in the hallway. So I got up and came to the door, where I took out my earplugs."

"So you left your compartment door open on purpose?" Hal persisted.

"I . . ." He cleared his throat and sat upright in the chair. "No, I must have left it open by accident."

"That's very helpful," said Erik, making a note. "One more thing—how do you know Mr. Crosby?"

"I don't know him, not really."

"But you indicated he knew you," Hal pointed out.

"Yes, well, it turns out I'm not important enough for Mr. Crosby to remember." Patrice grimaced. "But I can never forget him."

"What did he do that upset you?" Hal asked.

"He didn't *upset* me." Patrice leaned forward. "He tried to destroy my career."

"What happened?" Erik became interested.

"I was cast in a Hollywood movie produced by Crosgold, Mr. Crosby's company. It was meant to be my big break playing Tornado, the legendary boxer. I did six screen tests for that part, and when I got it, the producers asked me to gain weight for the role. I spent months eating eggs and red meat, drinking protein shakes and getting up at dawn for the gym, putting on forty pounds of solid muscle. After the first week of shooting, Mervyn Crosby visited the set in Los Angeles. Everyone was excited to meet the mogul behind the big movies, including me. He asked who I was playing, and when I said I was Tornado, he yelled, 'No, no, you're not, you're fired.' He shouted at the director: 'What are you doing casting this ogre? He'll look terrible on film—he's too big. Recast.'"

Patrice shrugged. "Then he just walked away. But I'd worked too hard for that part to let him throw my career in the trash. I ran after him and begged. He laughed at me, so I told him exactly what I thought of him." Patrice's lip curled. "He didn't like that. Security escorted me off the lot. Crosby put out the word I had a temper." He clenched his fists. "My agent dropped me, and I didn't work for two years. I still don't get cast outside South Africa. The man ruined my life, and it is so little to him that he does not even remember my name."

"And that makes you angry?" Erik asked.

"Of course it makes me angry." Patrice looked at Erik with a weary expression. "But I didn't kill him, if that's what you're implying. I am not so stupid, nor do I have so little self-control that I would let a man like that put me in a prison cell. His death is not worth my living."

"Did you know Mervyn Crosby was going to be on the Safari Star?"

"If I had known, I would not have come."

After Patrice had left, Winston let out a big sigh. "That was intense." He shook his head. "Patrice would've made a great Tornado. That movie was terrible."

"I think we should speak to Portia Ramaboa next," Erik announced.

Portia came into the compartment wearing a green-and-gold silk jacket and a wary expression. She perched on the edge of the chair as if she didn't intend to stay long.

"I was in the kitchen, speaking to the cook," she said, when Love- joy asked where she had been at the time of the shooting. Hal marked her on his diagram. "Mr. Leon, my dieti- cian, gave them specific requirements—

Portia Ramaboa

as everyone is now aware." She glanced at Hal, who squirmed. "I wanted to make sure that Mr. Ackerman's staff was preparing my evening meal correctly."

"In the service car?" asked Winston. "The one past the dining car?"

Portia nodded. "I was at the other end of the train. You saw me there yourself, Detective."

"Yes." Erik nodded. "I passed you in the corridor. You're quite right."

"Did you hear the shot?" asked Hal.

Portia shook her head. "It was too noisy—banging pots and pans, knives chopping. When I finished my conversation, I re- turned to Patrice so we could dress for dinner. As I approached our compartment, I saw people in the corridor. That was the first I knew about a shot."

"Patrice didn't want to come with you to the kitchen?"

Portia looked at Erik as if he'd said something stupid and shook her head. "Patrice was taking a nap."

"Does he often take naps?"

"Patrice is happiest when he's sleeping." She sounded proud, although her expression was mocking. "Like a lion in the sun."

"And you?"

"I did not become a prominent business leader by taking naps." She smiled.

"Had you met Mr. Crosby before?" asked Hal.

"No," said Portia. "But I knew his reputation, of course. They call him the great white shark. He is famous for his predatory business practices. But I had no particular reason to dislike him."

"What about Patrice?" Hal asked.

"Patrice hated Mervyn Crosby, with good reason. But I do not hold his grudges."

"Did you know the Crosbys were going to be on the Safari Star?" Erik asked.

Portia nodded. "I mentor Nicole Crosby. She told me."

"Is that why you bought a ticket?"

"It was one reason." Portia smiled. "Nicole had said she would like to meet me, and I thought a safari sounded romantic."

"But you didn't tell Patrice?" Hal thought that was a bit mean.

"Of course not. He would never have come. But I hoped the journey might help him lay an old demon to rest." She paused, hearing how that sounded, and gave Erik a half smile. "You know what I mean."

"I do." He nodded. "Thank you, Ms. Ramaboa. That's everything for now."

Hal frowned, thinking back to the argument he'd overheard between Portia and Patrice. She'd said, "There is more than your pride at stake here." As she rose to leave, he wrote the words in his sketchbook under her portrait, wondering what she'd meant by them.

"Her alibi is ironclad," said Erik after Portia had gone. "I saw her at the kitchens while I was getting myself some more fruit." He paused, reaching over and picking an emerald apple from the fruit platter and drawing a penknife from his pocket to peel it.

"There's something she's not telling us," Hal mused as Erik ate his apple. "I wonder what it is."

Beryl Brash entered in a whirl-wind of scarves. "Do your worst!" she exclaimed as she sat down, putting the back of her hand to her forehead. "Interrogate me!" She giggled. "Gosh, isn't this exciting?"

Hal smiled. He'd come to really like Beryl.

Beryl Brash

"A real-life murder on the Safari Star! You know, I was going to make one up, but at this rate my book will write itself." She clapped her hands down on her knees. "Come on, then. Ask me questions."

"We're conducting this investigation so that we can rule *out* murder," Erik said, turning to a new page of his notepad. "Where were you . . ."

"At the time of the murder? I'm glad you asked, because I know *exactly*. I was in my compartment, writing. There'd been so much wonderful drama at high tea, it really got my imagination flowing." She waggled her fingers on either side of her head. "Everybody was storming out, and I suddenly found myself alone in the observation car with Mervyn Crosby. And do you know what that ghastly man said to me? I was about to bite into my slice of fruit cake when he called across the room: 'I'm not sure that's a good idea for a lady of your size.'"

Hal was shocked. "What did you do?"

"I said, 'You're right. It's not a good idea. *It's a great idea.*' And I shoved the slice of cake into my mouth, grabbed my things, and walked out. The cheek of it! A man like him lecturing me? I'll have you know that I've written some of my best work powered by cake."

Hal grinned.

"Anyway, I was writing in my compartment with the window open, because I find the noise of air-conditioning very distracting, when I heard gunfire! I checked my watch, and it said three fifty-seven precisely. Of course, then I realized I hadn't changed my watch from London time, and I had to wind it forward. It was really five fifty-seven."

"Then what did you do?" Erik asked.

"I wrote about it."

"You wrote about it?"

"Yes! I turned to a fresh page and described the moment in detail so that I could put it in my book. Obviously, I didn't realize that a man had actually been killed. I thought it was divine providence. As I said—this book is writing itself!"

"Had you met Mr. Crosby before?" asked Hal.

"No," said Beryl, shaking her head. "Thank goodness. He's a vile man, or . . . he was. Oh dear, one mustn't speak ill of the dead." She lifted her eyebrows. "It makes one look guilty!"

Erik laughed, in spite of himself.

"Now . . ." Beryl rummaged in her handbag and pulled out her journal. "I'm sure you're going to ask if I think anyone on this train is suspicious, and I do. I think everyone is. The Sasakis talk to each other in Japanese, which nobody else understands. They could be saying anything! Or"—she licked a finger and flipped over the page—"how about Nicole Crosby? Did you know she's a vegetarian? Secretly she could be a member of an extremist animal rights group, who murdered her own father because he liked shooting endangered species, and then there's Nathaniel Bradshaw—"

"Are these plots for your book?" Winston asked.

"Why, yes! But any one of them could be true!"

Hal tried not to laugh.

"Would you be happy to loan us your journal, as evidence?" Erik asked.

"I'm afraid not." She put it back in her bag. "A writer's notebook is sacred."

There was a knock at the door. It was Amelia Crosby. She looked distressed, her mascara smudged as if she'd been rubbing her eyes. "I need to talk to you, Mr. Lovejoy."

"You're free to go, Beryl," Erik said, ushering her out of the room. "Although I may have more questions for you later." He winked at her, and she giggled. Closing the door, he turned to Amelia. "What is it?"

"It's Merv's shirts. They're missing."

"Missing?"

"I've moved into Nicole's compartment, and Mr. Ackerman had his staff bring our belongings from the Royal Suite. I've been going through them, packing Merv's things into a separate suitcase to ship them back to the States, but his shirts are missing. I just spoke with the attendants who cleared out the closet, and they say there were no shirts, but that's impossible. I packed five pink shirts for Merv, and he was wearing one when he . . . you know . . ." She couldn't bring herself to say it. "There should be four very expensive shirts for me to pack, but they're gone."

"How peculiar." Erik frowned. He looked at Hal and Winston. "Boys, let's take a break. I'll meet you back here in thirty minutes."

CHAPTER NINETEEN

ELEPHANT ON THE LINE

Being a deputy detective is hungry business," Winston said, picking up Chipo. "Shall we go to the kitchen and get a snack?"

As they arrived, Hal felt the train slowing down. "What's going on? Why are we stopping?" Hearing a long toot of the Safari Star's whistle, they opened the window, sticking their heads out.

"There's an elephant on the tracks!" Winston pointed.

The train slowed to a stop three or four yards away from the elephant, which was plodding calmly along the ballast.

Sheila blasted the train's whistle again.

Other heads popped out of windows as passengers and staff looked to see what was going on.

Hal saw Flo jump down from the train, followed by Liana, who went over to speak to her. Flo was pointing, and Liana was nodding.

"Let's go help them," Winston said.

"What are they going to do?"

"Drive the elephants back from the tracks. If there's one

elephant, there'll be others. We don't want to cause a stampede."
Winston was already at the door. "The Safari Star travels slowly
so you can see animals but also so it doesn't hurt them. Usually
the whistle scares them off the tracks, but if that doesn't work,
Mama moves them."

"How do you move an elephant?" Hal wondered.

Winston pointed. "Grab that silver tray. Come on."

Hal jumped down from the train, clutching the tray. He and
Winston hurried to join Khaya and two of the kitchen staff, who
were standing with Liana and Flo by the tender, armed with pans
and ladles.

"We'll ease Janice down the tracks at our slowest speed," Flo
said to Liana, "using the whistle at regular intervals."

Liana was nodding. "We'll try to drive the elephant back into
the trees."

Seeing Winston, Khaya smiled, handing him a frying pan and
wooden spoon.

"Where's Mr. Ackerman?" Hal said, looking about.

Flo's laugh was bitter. "My brother doesn't like hard work."
She exchanged a knowing look with Liana. "I take care of the
trains. Liana takes care of the animals. And Luther pretends to be
a passenger." She hoisted herself back into the engine cab to tell
Sheila and Greg the plan.

Hal followed the group as Liana directed them toward the
elephant using arm signals.

"Wait for me!" Over his shoulder, Hal saw Beryl picking her
way across the gravel. "I want to help!"

Everyone started banging their pots and pans. Having nothing
to bang his tray with, Hal slipped off his shoe and joined in the

merry din-making. Beryl clapped her hands together and made wailing noises as if she were a ghost, and Hal laughed and wailed, too. The Safari Star's whistle sounded in bursts and the locomotive crawled forward at walking pace.

In this way the train carefully passed the elephants, and Hal waved at Uncle Nat, who was leaning out of a window, gazing at the herd half hidden among the trees.

Once they were back on board, the boys ran to the lounge, where Uncle Nat was sitting with his journal in his lap.

"Did you see us move the elephant?" Hal gabbled excitedly.

Uncle Nat nodded. "I wish I could have joined you, but my ankle's bothering me today." He wrinkled his nose. "It feels a bit tender."

"Are you writing?" Hal nodded at the journal.

"No, actually, I've been reading up on the Safari Star." He pointed to the bookcase. "Some of these carriages were manufactured a hundred years ago in Belgium, by the International Sleeping Car Company. They were designed for the Orient Express, in the years before the Second World War. I wouldn't be surprised if they were filled with secret hiding places to help move documents and contraband across borders."

"Cool!" Hal and Winston looked at each other with delight.

"To tell you the truth, I'm a bit envious of your detective work with Erik. Have you uncovered any secrets?"

"We discovered Patrice hated Mr. Crosby because he made him eat loads of eggs and steaks and ruined his career," Winston said.

"I beg your pardon?" Uncle Nat blinked.

"Winston! We're not supposed to tell anyone what people say in the interview room, remember?"

"But it's your uncle," Winston protested.

"We have to get back," Hal said. "It's already been half an hour."

"I'll come with you." Uncle Nat got up. "Erik might want to interview me next."

The three of them returned to the compartment, which Winston insisted on calling the interrogation room.

"What are you doing here, Nathaniel?" Erik said.

"I'm ready for my interview," Uncle Nat announced, sitting on the chair. "I don't want any preferential treatment just because we're old friends."

Erik scratched his head. "I wasn't going to interview you. I don't really need to." He pointed at the boys. "Between the three of us, we know exactly where you were the whole time, and you don't have a motive for killing Mr. Crosby, so . . ." He shrugged. "I was only going to call you in at the end, to corroborate other people's alibis."

"Ah. I see. But I'm sure I can help somehow." He paused to think. "Did Hal and Winston go through our reconstruction with you?"

Erik leaned over the table as Hal explained the entrances, exits, and hiding places they'd observed in their suite. "You really think there would have been time for someone to leave Mr. Crosby's compartment while you were inside Patrice's room?"

"Maybe," Hal said, "but someone would have bumped into them farther on down the corridor."

"There's one unoccupied suite before the lounge," said Uncle Nat, pointing to Hal's diagram of the train. "Could someone have hidden in there?"

"It would've been locked," Winston said.

"Interesting." Erik made a note. "And this . . . wire trick you did with the connecting door." He pointed at the sketch. "How long did that take you to construct?"

"Only a few seconds," said Hal. "Oh! We wanted to ask you about Mr. Crosby's compartment key—was it still there when you searched the room?"

"It was on his desk."

Hal added a key to the diagram.

"That rules out anyone using Mr. Crosby's key to escape." Uncle Nat sighed.

"You've been very helpful, Nathaniel," Erik said. "But if I'm going to get through everyone before lunch, I must speak to the Sasakis."

Uncle Nat looked crestfallen, but he wished them luck as he left the compartment.

"He's so jealous of us being deputies," Winston whispered to Hal with a giggle.

Hal nodded, feeling a flash of guilt.

"I hope you don't mind speaking to us together, Detective," Ryo Sasaki said as he and Satsuki sat down. "Satsuki is worried she might not be able to answer all your questions without me here to help translate."

"Not at all, Mr. Sasaki," Erik replied, smiling at Satsuki. "This won't take long. Let's start with where you were at the time of Mervyn Crosby's death."

"We were in our suite, together," said Ryo. "We went there after the unpleasant scenes at high tea."

Satsuki and Ryo Sasaki

Satsuki said something to him in Japanese and pointed to the window.

"Yes." He turned to Erik. "We were watching a raptor riding a thermal above the train." He demonstrated the bird in flight with his hand. "Majestic."

"You were there when the shot was fired?"

"Yes, I heard the gun. I looked out the window to see if Mr. Crosby was shooting at the bird, but saw nothing. I automatically picked up my medical bag and went to investigate. I heard Mr. Bradshaw shouting for me when I arrived."

"What did you do after your husband left, Mrs. Sasaki?"

"I went to the lounge," Satsuki replied, "to choose a book."

When asked whether they knew Mr. Crosby, Ryo replied that they had not met him before but repeated the story about the super casino Mr. Crosby was trying to build in Kyoto. "But I am certain Mr. Crosby has never set foot in Kyoto," he added.

Satsuki said something, and Ryo replied sternly.

"What was that?" Erik asked.

Ryo cleared his throat. "Satsuki says Mr. Crosby's death is . . . good for Kyoto."

Nobody disagreed. Having asked all his questions, Erik said they could leave. A moment later, there was a knock, and Liana stood in the doorway.

"Mama!" Winston waved, and Chipo rose onto his haunches.

"They're not causing any trouble?" she asked Erik.

"On the contrary. They're very helpful."

"I know you haven't called me, but there is something I want to talk to you about."

"Come in. Sit down."

Liana Tsotsobe

Liana pulled an envelope from her pocket and slid out a white card. "Yesterday afternoon, I went to my compartment during high tea, to take a break from the passengers, and I found this note. It's from Mervyn Crosby." She passed it to him.

"'Meet me in the dining car at a quarter to six. MC,'" Erik read aloud. "Hmm." He looked at Liana, as Hal scribbled down the words in his sketchbook. "Do you know what Mr. Crosby wanted to talk to you about?"

Liana shrugged. "I would like to think he wanted to apologize to me, although it doesn't seem likely." She sighed. "My job is to answer questions and talk to the guests, so I went to the dining car and waited. He never showed, of course. Later I found out he was dead."

"So at the time of his death you were in the dining car? Did anyone see you there?"

"Yes, Khaya and I talked while I was waiting."

"Would you mind if I kept this?" Erik held up the card. "It could be important."

161

Liana agreed, warned Winston to be good, and left. Then it was Luther Ackerman's turn.

Luther Ackerman

"Is this necessary?" He hurried to the interview chair, glancing about anxiously. "I'm very busy."

"We are establishing a timeline, to check everybody's alibis," Erik replied. "Where were you at the time of the shooting?"

"I'm not exactly sure, because I didn't hear it. I was moving a heavy chair from the lounge into an empty compartment. A guest had complained that it looked tatty and that it offended them."

"Which guest?" Hal asked.

"Amelia Crosby." He looked at Erik. "I'd just got it through the door when Nathaniel Bradshaw came running up the corridor saying that Mervyn Crosby was about to shoot a rhinoceros from his compartment! I left the chair and ran after him."

"He only had that gun because you let him keep it," Hal said. "If you'd confiscated it like you said, this wouldn't have happened."

"He said he wouldn't use it!" Ackerman wailed. "I couldn't . . . He's *Mervyn Crosby*! His newspapers are powerful. If he'd enjoyed himself, people would flock to our railway. But if he didn't"—he shook his head, his mouth open—"he could have ruined my reputation! Things haven't been easy the past few years. The railway isn't getting the bookings it once did."

"I need to ask you about Mr. Crosby's shirts," Erik said, changing the subject.

"I know!" Luther clapped his hands to his face. "They've disappeared." He shook his head. "Why does nothing ever go right for me?" He threw his hands in the air. "One of the staff must've taken them. I asked the attendants who cleared the compartment. They all swear there were no shirts in the wardrobe. It's a mystery."

"Hmm." Erik wrote in his notebook. "Can you tell me the whereabouts of all the crew at the time of Mr. Crosby's death?"

"No one was at that end of the train—I've checked. Everyone was where they should have been. If you come to my office, I'll give you the shift sheet and you can ask them yourself."

"That would be helpful." Erik nodded. "One last thing, Luther, and then you can go. Mr. Crosby's compartment was locked. Who else had a key to it?"

"Only me," said Ackerman. "I have keys to all the compartments. Housekeeping uses my master set. They pick up the keys first thing and return them when the rooms are turned down during breakfast."

"Thank you, that's—"

But the nervous train manager left before Erik could finish telling him he was free to go.

"Anyone else think he was being weird?" Hal asked.

"Yes, but your uncle is his alibi, which puts him in the middle of the train at the time of the shooting," Erik pointed out. "And he's nothing to gain from Crosby's death. In fact, quite the opposite."

"Everyone else seems better off, though," Hal said, staring down at his sketches of the suspects. "Some people don't have strong alibis, but even then . . ." He sighed. "No one could have known Mr. Crosby would think he saw a rhino at that exact moment and be ready to rush to his cabin to grab his gun."

"And if there was a struggle for the gun, why didn't we hear it?" asked Winston.

"You're right," said Erik. "It seems impossible that he shot himself, but also impossible that he didn't."

CHAPTER TWENTY

THE BULAWAYO BREAKTHROUGH

There was a knock at the interrogation-room door, and Khaya entered with an envelope. "Detective Lovejoy? I have the printouts you asked for."

"What's that?" Hal asked.

"The forensic report from the examination of Mr. Crosby's compartment. I asked for it to be sent to me when it was completed." Erik opened the envelope and took out a wad of paper, his eyes skimming the sheets as he read them at speed. Hal looked at the pages, filled with tables and dense text with long words, and realized that being a real police officer was hard work.

"Well . . ." Erik sighed as he finished the last page. "I'm not sure that helps us."

"What does it say?" Winston asked.

"In summary, the only fingerprints found in the room and on the gun belonged to Mr. and Mrs. Crosby. The type of bullet that killed Mervyn Crosby matches the bullets for his rifle. One shot was fired from the rifle. And after a thorough search, they found no evidence that would question the police's assessment that his death was a tragic accident."

"Oh," Hal felt deflated. "But what about the missing shirts?"

"I think Mr. Ackerman's right. One of the staff must have fancied them." He shrugged. "Mr. Crosby no longer needs them, does he?"

Winston grimaced. "I wouldn't want to walk around in a dead man's shirt."

Erik rubbed his hands over his face. "Right, I think we should get Amelia in here and go through the facts."

Hal and Winston sat down behind their table as Erik welcomed Amelia into the compartment.

"We'd like to take you through the case," Erik explained. "Firstly, let's consider our suspects. Harrison, what do we have on Patrice Mbatha?"

"A few minutes after the shot, Winston and I crept into his cabin and saw him fast asleep in bed. The connecting door between the compartments was locked on both sides. He holds a grudge against Mr. Crosby, so has a motive, but it's unlikely he could have killed him because he had no way of knowing your husband would return to his compartment at that moment in time."

Erik nodded. "And his fingerprints weren't found on the weapon."

"Portia Ramaboa has an alibi: she was in the kitchen talking to the chef," Hal went on.

"I saw her myself, which makes her my alibi," Erik said, nodding again. "And she doesn't have a motive. At the time of Mr. Crosby's death, Luther Ackerman can be placed in the lounge car,

Nathaniel Bradshaw was running down the corridor toward him, Liana Tsotsobe was sitting in the dining car talking to Khaya, and Mr. and Mrs. Sasaki were in their compartment together bird-watching. I myself saw Ryo appear in the corridor from that direction once we'd got the door to your suite open. Hal and Winston were outside the door, and Nicole was in the bath, as vouched for by you."

"So who doesn't have an alibi?" Amelia frowned.

"The only people who don't have alibis are Beryl Brash . . ." He took a breath. "And you."

"Me?"

"You stated that Nicole got in the bath and was still in there when I asked you both to join me in the dining car. However, once she got in the bath, she heard only the TV on for the next forty-five minutes. Not you."

"I see."

"Beryl Brash was in her cabin when she was called to the lounge with the other guests. It would have been difficult for her to have traveled up the train and back without being seen, but not impossible. However, she doesn't have a key for your compartment and none of her fingerprints were found there." Erik brought his hands together. "So you see: taking into account alibis, our only possible suspects are Beryl and you. And though Beryl didn't like your husband, she doesn't have a strong motive for murder."

"I wouldn't kill Merv."

"Or, if you did, you would've been delighted by the police's assessment of the situation and you would have accepted it. You wouldn't have asked me to investigate." He looked at Hal and Winston. "What do you think?"

Amelia turned to Hal, an expectant look on her face.

"All of the evidence points in one direction," Hal said. "No one could have known Mr. Crosby would run to get his gun exactly at that moment. I was with him on the veranda—one minute he was talking about how much fun it would be to shoot impala, and then he saw the rhino and ran off. The room was locked from the inside. The bullet that killed him came from his own gun, and the only fingerprints in the room and on the weapon were his and yours."

"You think it was an accident?" Erik prompted.

"I do." Hal nodded. "Either he dropped the gun and it misfired, or he shot out the window and the bullet ricocheted off a rock and hit him."

Amelia looked suddenly relieved. "So Nic is safe?"

Erik nodded, and she let out a little laugh. "Who'd have thought it? Merv killed by his own gun! Thank you, Detective Lovejoy, and you, too, Harrison and Winston. You've made me feel much safer." She stood up. "I'm really free!" She looked astonished. "I suppose I'd better go and get changed for this afternoon's safari."

"Good work, boys," Erik said after she'd gone. He stacked the pages from the forensics report and slid them back in the envelope.

"We didn't catch a murderer," Winston said, sounding disappointed.

"The job is to solve the case." Erik walked to the door. "I'm going to pop by Luther's office and get that staff shift sheet and make sure everything checks out, and then take a bath. See you on safari."

"I'd better go," said Winston. "I'm helping Mama at the Hwange reserve. Being a deputy detective is fun, but being a safari ranger is better." He helped Chipo onto his shoulder, then looked back at Hal, who was still sitting at the table. "What's up?"

"I don't know," Hal said, getting to his feet. "It's just . . . when I've solved cases before, it felt different."

"How?"

"There's always been this moment—it's hard to describe. Like all the jigsaw pieces fall from the sky and land in place, making a perfect picture of what happened." He looked at Winston. "I don't feel that this time."

"Maybe because this time there hasn't been a crime."

"Maybe." Hal nodded, but he had an unnerving feeling that wasn't it.

***

Back at their compartment, Uncle Nat was working at the table. Hal pulled up a chair and opened his sketchbook.

"Did you solve the case?"

"It was an accident, like the police said." Hal took out his charcoal tin, selected a stick, and began to draw. He worked away in silence, thinking of Satsuki and how origami calmed her. The train was traveling at an unhurried pace as they trundled past a redbrick building with a sign reading BULAWAYO STATION.

"The heart of Zimbabwe's railways." Uncle Nat sighed, and Hal guessed he would have liked to get off and explore. But the train kept moving.

"What're you working on?" Uncle Nat pointed at the sketchbook.

"Not sure. I'm drawing moments from the journey, hoping it will jog something or make a connection."

"I thought you said Crosby's death was an accident."

"All the evidence points that way, but something doesn't feel right. I'm missing something."

"Best keep drawing, then." Uncle Nat nodded.

Hal put down the charcoal. "What if I only feel this way because I'd *really like* there to be a crime?"

"How about you give your mind a rest? Forget about being a detective for a bit, and get dressed for our game drive in Hwange. I'm not sure I'll be doing much walking about because of my ankle, but I plan to sit in our Jeep and marvel."

"I'll stay with you this time," Hal said, thinking of his brush with the black mamba. "For the rest of the day I'm only going to draw animals."

CHAPTER TWENTY-ONE

DEAD STRAIGHT

When Hal came out of the bathroom dressed in his khakis, he found Uncle Nat kneeling on a chair, hanging his head out of the window like a dog. "Hal, look at this!" he said, waving him over.

Hal stuck his head out the window, too, blinking as wind and coal smuts buffeted his face.

"We're on the second-longest stretch of straight track in the world. It's called the Dete straight and goes all the way from Gwai to Dete. That's more than a hundred kilometers of track without a bend."

Hal looked up at his uncle's happy face.

"You have to lean right out to see the side of the locomotive." Uncle Nat did just that, and Hal copied him, the pair grinning at each other, whooping like a train whistle. Hal looked behind them to where the track was straight as a ruler, vanishing into the distance like a pin.

Before long, the Safari Star pulled off the main line and into a siding. Hal and Uncle Nat jumped down from the train into the heat of the afternoon, ambling toward the engine. The track cut like a scar through the green trees. The click and slam of carriage doors behind them shattered the gentle chorus of crickets and bugs stridulating away in the undergrowth.

"How's Janice?" Uncle Nat called out as Flo and Greg clambered down the ladder from the footplate.

"Doing well," Flo replied. "Don't touch her, though. She's so hot she'll take the skin off your hand. Once she's cooled, we'll carry out her mechanical checks, make sure she'll get us to Victoria Falls safely."

"Why is she called Janice?" Hal asked, thinking it was an odd name for an engine.

"It was the name of the original driver's wife," Flo replied.

Hal pictured his dad naming a train Beverly and grinned.

Sheila was scrambling over the roof of the tender with a water hose. She lifted a hatch and fed it in, giving the thirsty Janice a long, cool drink.

Satsuki, Ryo, Portia, and Patrice had gathered in the shade of the tender. Liana strode over, followed by Winston and Chipo. "Is that everyone?" she asked, as Erik helped Beryl down from the train.

"Almost," replied Uncle Nat, and they all turned to watch two of the train crew hurrying to a door, carrying wooden planks to lay on the ground.

"Don't worry," Nicole said as she jumped down, wearing sneakers, jean shorts, and a T-shirt. "We can manage." Hal blinked with surprise as Amelia Crosby stepped lightly from the train, dressed in walking boots, survival pants, and a short-sleeved, camouflage-patterned shirt tied in a knot at her waist.

She looked a far cry from the glamorous doll who had boarded the train in Pretoria. Her hair was held back from her face by an olive headscarf, and she wore no makeup.

"Hi," Nicole said shyly.

"Hello." Hal sensed she was embarrassed about crying in her interview, so he beamed at her to try to show support.

"Are you okay?" Nicole asked.

"I was trying to look friendly."

"You always look friendly."

"I do?" Hal blushed.

"This way," Liana called out. "We've a short walk ahead of us. Please watch your step." She led the group away from the train, down a winding path through the trees. The canopy served as a parasol, shading them from the sun, and Hal felt relief at the drop in temperature.

"Thanks for looking into what happened to Pop," Nicole said, falling into step beside him. "Mom was freaking out, saying that someone was after us for our money. I was really scared. It's a relief to know it definitely was an accident."

Hal felt uncomfortable. In his gut, he wasn't entirely sure it *was* an accident. What if there was more to Mr. Crosby's death than they knew?

"Talk about ironic, right?" Nicole said. "He brought down so many big animals with that gun and the last one was himself!"

"Mm-hm." Hal nodded.

"Maybe it's just karma," Nicole continued. "D'you know, every Thanksgiving, Pop would tell us this story at the dinner table, about how when he was my age and living in Joburg, he stole a car, picked up his best friend, and drove it around town all night. When the police caught them, Pop ran off, letting his friend take the fall. He even went to prison." She shook her head with disgust. "But Pop would say, 'Listen, Nic—it's okay to break the law, as long as you don't get caught. That's the secret to *winning*. Never getting caught . . .'"

Hal stopped walking and stared at her. "That's awful!"

"I know. He'd raise a glass and give thanks that so many people were suckers." She grimaced. "He was an awful person. I'm surprised someone *didn't* try to kill him."

"Mm." Hal nodded, a wave of panic building in his chest.

"I mean," Nicole mused, "what's the likelihood that a person so many people hated would do the world a favor and accidentally kill himself? That's what Mom said, anyway. She was really

relieved when you explained it couldn't have been anything but an accident. Pop was so good with guns, but I guess even trained shooters make mistakes."

"Where's Uncle Nat?" Hal said abruptly. "I should be helping him."

Nicole nodded, and Hal hurried back to his uncle's side. *What if we're wrong?* he thought. *What if Mr. Crosby was murdered and the killer is still on the train? What if Nicole's in danger?*

Uncle Nat smiled gratefully as Hal took his hand and put it on his shoulder, so he could lean on him as he limped through the trees. They reached a wide clearing where a low wooden building was stationed discreetly in the undergrowth. The guests followed Liana inside to a lounge furnished with wood and stone. Folding doors in a large glass wall opened onto a balcony, which over-looked a pool of water fed by a waterfall, surrounded by tall trees and lush vegetation.

"Welcome to the Lodge," Liana said. "This is our base for this afternoon. If you wish, you may relax here and look at the animals that visit the pan"—she indicated the watering hole—"or come with me for an excursion deeper into the game park. This evening we will all meet back here for dinner on the veranda."

Winston came over, Chipo lying across his shoulders like a scarf. "You're coming on the game drive, right?"

"Sure. I think Mom's planning on staying, though," Nicole said. "I'll go check."

"*Winston*," Hal hissed as she walked away. "What if we've got it wrong?"

"Got what wrong?"

"What if Mr. Crosby *was* murdered?"

"But . . ."

"I know what we said, but our theory doesn't *feel* right. It's too easy—Nicole just said so herself! What if someone's gotten away with the perfect murder? What if they killed him and made it look like an accident?"

"Who?"

"*I don't know!*" Hal whispered desperately. "But Nicole could still be in danger." He looked about nervously.

"Hal, you're panicking."

"*Of course I'm panicking!*"

"Stroke Chipo. She'll calm you down." Winston twisted so Hal could reach the mongoose. "What do you think we should do?"

"Stay close to Nicole and keep her safe," Hal said. "She can't know we think there might be a killer on the loose. We don't want to frighten her."

"Okay." Winston looked doubtful. "But what are you going to do about this killer?"

"Keep drawing and stay calm."

"Right." Winston shot him a questioning look. "Drawing."

"Winston!" Liana called out. "Please get everyone to the Jeep. It's time for the game drive."

CHAPTER TWENTY-TWO

THE GAME DRIVE

Only Patrice and Portia joined Uncle Nat, Hal, and Nicole on the game drive. Hal stuck beside Nicole as they followed Winston and Liana to the open-topped Jeep. Portia and Patrice took the back seats, Nicole got into the middle row, and Uncle Nat's eyebrows rose as Hal sat beside her, leaving him on his own in the front. Winston climbed into the passenger seat beside his mother. He was wearing his rucksack back to front, strapped to his chest like a papoose, with Chipo's head peeping out of the top.

Hal relaxed when he realized that the only person in the Jeep without a proper alibi for the murder was Patrice. It would be easy enough to keep an eye on him.

"Hwange National Park is the largest nature reserve in Zimbabwe," Liana said as they drove slowly along a dirt track through the trees. "It is home to over a hundred species of mammal and four hundred types of bird."

"Hal, where's your sketchbook?" Uncle Nat had his binoculars to his eyes and was peering up at the canopy. "You said you wanted to draw animals."

"Yes, that's right." Hal smiled at Nicole as he took out his sketchbook and tin of charcoal, trying to appear relaxed. "I love drawing animals."

"Ooh, is that . . . ?" Uncle Nat lifted his head. "It is! Look, up there, a racket-tailed roller! Do you see it, Hal? The bird with the turquoise breast and those circular ends to its tail feathers."

Hal spotted the bird too late to put much more than a line on the page. The details of the Crosby case were bubbling in his brain, distracting him.

When the Jeep emerged from the trees, it was onto a wide, dusty plane where wispy grasses grew in broad clumps. Uncle Nat put on his panama hat to shade his face, and Hal saw that his nose was peeling.

"We're heading for that pan," Liana called out. "There's a watering hole where we should find some animals."

"What's a pan?" Hal asked. It was the second time he'd heard her use the word that afternoon.

"A hollow in the ground where water collects, like a big frying pan," Uncle Nat replied, passing back his binoculars. "Look over by the acacia tree, on the right."

It took Hal a moment to focus the lenses, but then he saw a long, golden-spotted neck, and the head of a giraffe munching a mouthful of leaves from the top of the tree.

"Giraffes have really big teeth," Hal marveled. "And look how long its tongue is!"

"A giraffe's tongue is as long as a human arm," Winston said. "They can curl it backward and use it to clean their own ears. Look, there are more giraffes behind that one, camouflaged by the trees."

Liana took them as close as she safely could, stopped the Jeep, and turned off the engine.

Hal got to work, drawing the regal lines of the giraffes' faces, as they milled around in a time frame slower than the rest of the world. They had dark, soulful eyes, and their strange furry horns made them look like friendly aliens.

With a slow, graceful stride, one of the giraffes approached the water's edge, splaying its front legs inelegantly as it dipped its head to drink. "Why's it doing that?" Hal asked Winston.

"A giraffe's neck is too short to reach the ground. They get most of the water they need from the leaves they eat. They have to do that weird thing with their legs if they want to drink."

"Over there!" Patrice said, pointing to the opposite bank.

"Zebras!" Portia whispered, leaning forward, her face momentarily girlish.

"Do you know the collective noun for zebras?" Uncle Nat asked Hal.

"It's a dazzle," Portia replied. "A *dazzle* of zebras."

"That's perfect," Nicole said, smiling. In that look, Hal could see how much she admired Portia. She must be a good mentor, he thought, and he wondered if Uncle Nat was his.

"Yeah, but it's a *tower* of giraffes," Winston said.

"Dazzle is better," Nicole teased.

Gazing across the watering hole, Hal picked a zebra and drew the graceful curve of its back. He'd not taken much time to consider the relationships between the people on the train. He'd been so fixated on the puzzle of the locked room, on the possible and impossible, that he'd ignored how people were connected. His mind whirled as he drew the zebra's many lines onto the paper.

What if two people had committed the murder? He realized with a shock that he'd been assuming it was only one. Good detectives didn't make assumptions or jump to conclusions, and he'd done both.

"There are three species

of zebra," Winston said. "Those are the plain zebra. Each zebra's stripe pattern is unique. That's how they recognize one another."

"Like a barcode," Uncle Nat said to Hal, his smile replaced with curiosity as he read Hal's face.

As the sun started to sink, Liana turned their Jeep round. They bounced back along the uneven track toward the Lodge, and it was twilight by the time they parked beside it. The sky was a kaleidoscope of pinks and purples.

"I don't like the look of those," said Uncle Nat, pointing at distant clouds the color of tar.

"There's a storm coming," said Liana, parking and turning off the engine. "You can feel it in the air."

Inside the Lodge, a long table had been laid with a buffet of peanut-butter rice, sardines, *sadza* (a savory porridge dish), a mix of greens, and a selection of barbecued pork ribs, steak, and roadrunner chicken.

"What's this?" Hal asked Winston.

"Meat stew with mopane worms," Winston replied, dishing himself up a portion. "It's really good."

Hal added a ladle of the stew to his rice and took a leg of chicken, following everyone out to the balcony, which was lit by flickering torches and floodlights.

"Perhaps the rain will give us some relief from this heat." Beryl sighed, fanning herself with a napkin.

"I'm going to enjoy the last bit of the journey, whatever the weather," Erik replied. "Now that the Crosby case is closed."

"I'm disappointed it didn't turn out to be a gruesome murder," Beryl admitted in a low voice. "It would've been much more thrilling."

Erik laughed.

Hal studied Beryl. She had no alibi, but he hadn't seriously considered her as a suspect. She wrote murder mysteries for a living—had she come up with some ingenious way of killing Mr. Crosby?

A metallic-green beetle landed on Satsuki Sasaki's arm as she propped her plate on the balcony's railings. She watched it crawl to her hand, then along her middle finger, where it paused, gleaming like a giant emerald ring, before flicking out its elytra and launching itself into the air. She seemed an unlikely murderer to Hal: She had such respect for nature. But would she kill to protect it? Or even help her husband do it? Ryo Sasaki had been the first to examine Mr. Crosby's body after the shooting. Hal remembered him pulling on his surgical gloves. It was very convenient that he'd had his gloves and medical bag at the ready. Had he worn them to avoid leaving fingerprints at the crime scene?

Winston sat next to Hal, holding a plate heaped with food. "Not hungry?"

Chipo jumped into his lap and helped herself to a lump of papaya.

"Are you still trying to work out who the murderer is?" he whispered.

Hal nodded. "I wish I could have seen into the compartment after Mr. Crosby was shot. It's hard to try to solve a murder that you didn't see."

"You still could."

"See the murder?"

"No, you fruit bat." Winston rolled his eyes. "Examine the

crime scene. We could do it now." He looked around. "While everyone is here, eating."

"We'd have to watch out for Mr. Ackerman."

"I think we can outsmart old Ackerman." Winston grinned.

"Mind if I join you?" Uncle Nat said, and they both looked up. "Uh-oh! I've seen that face before." He sat down beside Hal. "What's going on?"

"You know how drawing helps me think?"

Uncle Nat nodded.

"Well, I've been thinking I might have been wrong about Mr. Crosby's death being an accident. I can't really explain why. I have a powerful feeling here"—he put his hand to his chest—"and it's not a good one."

"I see."

"I need to get a look at Mr. Crosby's compartment, and right now, with everyone off the train, this is the best chance I'll get."

Winston's eyes widened, unable to believe Hal was telling his uncle their plan.

"I'll come with you," said Uncle Nat at once.

"No." Hal fixed his uncle with a serious look. "Your ankle will slow us down. We need to get to the train quickly. And if there is a murderer here, Nicole might be in danger."

"I won't leave her side." Uncle Nat nodded. "But you must promise to be careful."

"I promise," Hal said, handing him his plate of food.

The two boys ducked out of the Lodge, running down the dusty path back to the Safari Star. Distant thunder rumbled through the shadowy trees, and Hal suddenly felt very glad to have Winston with him.

CHAPTER TWENTY-THREE

ROOFTOP DROP

The silhouette of the Safari Star loomed in the twilight as they hurried back along the path. Sensing the coming storm, the invisible chorus of creatures in the trees had fallen eerily silent, and Chipo cowered in her rucksack.

"How are we going to get in?" Hal asked as they approached the train. "The police locked the compartment." Lights shone from the service cars and Mr. Ackerman's room, but the rest of the train was dark.

"Mr. Crosby's window," Winston suggested. "It might still be open."

The boys hurried round the end of the train.

"It is," Hal said excitedly as they ran toward it. "No one's closed it." He jumped to see if he could reach it, but he wasn't tall enough.

"Here." Winston made a cradle with his hands. "Try with a bunk up."

Hal tried several times, but the window was a fraction too high for his fingers to reach the frame. "It's no good." He dropped to the ground. "We'll have to find another way."

185

"What about the roof?" Winston looked up. "We could lower ourselves in."

"Great idea." Hal grinned.

They clambered up to the observation-car veranda. Winston shifted his rucksack from his chest to his back, zipping Chipo inside. Hal watched as he climbed onto the balcony railings,

heaving himself up onto the roof, legs kicking. The wind ruffled Hal's shirt as he followed behind, rolling onto the rooftop, still warm from the evening sun.

"Come on," said Winston, keeping low and running softly over the top of the carriage. As they jumped the gap to the first sleeping car, there was a bright flash. Hal looked up. The red and smoky clouds in the distance were severed by hairline cracks of lightning, and a moment later thunder rolled over the treetops.

"Rain's coming," Winston called out. "Quick." He crouched down. "Grab the mushroom vent with one hand and lower your legs over the edge. I'll hold your arms, so you don't fall."

Hal grabbed the vent and slid his legs over the edge of the carriage. He felt a dart of fear, but Winston gripped his wrists firmly. His dangling legs found the open window, and he released one hand, grabbing the frame and pulling himself into Mr. Crosby's compartment, falling to the floor in a heap.

Winston came through the window behind him, landing on his feet with a wobble. "We did it!" He grinned at Hal.

A flash of lightning lit up the compartment, and they both stopped smiling as they saw the dark bloodstain on the carpet.

"Shut the blind. I'll turn that lamp on," Hal whispered. "We don't want anyone to know we're here." He took out his sketchbook, noticing Mr. Crosby's key on the desk.

Winston unzipped his rucksack. Chipo's head popped out, and she touched her nose to his.

"We'll start at one end of the compartment and work our way to the other, looking for anything that might tell us what happened." Hal went into the bathroom. "Whoa! You weren't lying about the Jacuzzi."

Finding nothing in the bathroom, the boys worked backward, checking under the bed, behind the bedside table, in the desk drawers and wastepaper bin, but found nothing until Hal opened the wardrobe. "Hey, what's this?" With his fingernails, he teased out a scrap of pink cloth trapped in the hinge of the door.

"Is it a clue?" Winston asked, excitedly.

"I don't know," Hal admitted. "It might be."

"Do you think the murderer jumped out the wardrobe to attack Mr. Crosby, and caught his shirt on the door?"

"Mervyn Crosby was shot from the front, with his own gun. Remember Uncle Nat getting inside our wardrobe? He could barely fit. Also, this is pink. It must be from one of Mr. Crosby's own shirts."

"We still don't know why they went missing."

"Or who has them now." Hal laid the scrap of cloth between two pages of his sketchbook. The origami owl Satsuki had made him slipped out, floating to the floor of the wardrobe. Hal reached in to pick it up and noticed a groove in the wood that didn't match the grain. He ran his finger along it and spontaneously pushed down. It moved, and he heard a click. "Winston!" He gasped as a small panel opened at the back of the wardrobe.

"A secret compartment!" Winston whispered.

"It's empty." Hal sighed, reaching in and feeling around. "No—wait. What's this? Can you lift that lamp and point the light through the door?" Winston brought the lamp as far as its cable would stretch. "There's some dirt and a lump of something gray. Like an old tooth, or a bit of rock." Hal carefully picked it up, placing it on the palm of his hand. "Look." He turned round to show Winston.

Winston pointed the lamp at Hal's hand, and the boys stared at the odd-looking fragment. Then Winston reached into his pocket and pulled out a magnifying glass, peering at the curious lump. His face fell.

"What is it?" Hal asked. "What's wrong?"

"We have to find my mother," Winston said quietly. "Hal—I think this is *rhino horn*."

CHAPTER TWENTY-FOUR

OPERATION HURRICANE

Winston grabbed an envelope from the desk, and Hal tipped the fragment into it.

"We shouldn't talk to anyone about this until we've shown Mama."

Hal nodded, unlocking the compartment door with Mr. Crosby's key, then locking it behind them and sliding the key underneath. His mind raced as Winston led them wordlessly toward the service cars. *Why was there a rhino horn in Mr. Crosby's compartment? Was he a smuggler? Was that why he was murdered?*

As they passed through the dark lounge, Hal saw passengers walking back from the Lodge, lanterns swinging at their sides to guide their way. "They're coming back."

Hal and Winston waited for Liana in her compartment, sitting side by side on the bottom bunk.

The door slid open, and Liana came in, dumping her duffel bag on the floor. "What's wrong, *nunu?*" she asked. "Why are your clothes dirty?"

190

"We were doing some investigating." Winston passed her the envelope. "We found this."

She opened it, took out the fragment, and examined it, turning on the light so she could see it clearly. "Where did you get this?" Her voice was a whisper.

"It was in a secret compartment at the back of Mr. Crosby's wardrobe," Hal said.

Liana looked stunned. "Have you told anybody else?"

"We came straight to you," Winston said. "Mama . . . is it rhino horn?"

A crack of thunder finally unleashed the rain, arriving in sheets that rattled the roof of the train.

"It doesn't look like anything special," Hal said.

"It's not ivory," Liana replied. "Rhino horns are keratin all the way through, they don't have a core of bone. The weight and texture are about right."

"Keratin?" Hal looked at Winston.

"It's the stuff your fingernails and hair are made from," he explained.

"We must take this to Detective Lovejoy," Liana declared. "This is serious. Rhino-horn smuggling is a terrible crime."

The three of them marched to Erik's compartment, and he opened the door, buttoning up a cotton shirt. "Hello, it's my deputy detectives." He smiled. "Listen to that rain!" He saw Liana's grave expression. "What's wrong?"

Closing the door behind them, Liana handed the envelope to Erik. "The boys have found a piece of rhino horn in Mr. Crosby's room."

Erik stared at Hal and Winston in wonder. "But the police forensics team went through it with a fine-tooth comb. They found nothing."

"It was in a secret compartment, behind the false back of the wardrobe," Hal said.

"I think someone on this train may be dealing with smugglers," Liana said gravely. "You and I both know how dangerous they are. That's why we're bringing this to you now, instead of waiting and going to the police tomorrow morning."

Erik let out a long sigh. "Sit down, you three. There's something I need to tell you."

Hal and Winston perched on one armchair, while Liana took the other.

"I'm going to tell you something that I'd not intended to share with anyone on this train. You must promise me you won't tell another soul until our journey has ended. It could jeopardize everything."

Winston and Liana nodded, murmuring their agreement.

"Hal?"

"I don't like hiding things from my uncle."

Erik smiled. "You can tell Nathaniel." He pointed his finger. "But only him."

"I promise." Hal nodded, relieved.

"I am not a retired police detective." Erik sat back. "I'm an active member of the department, working undercover on a live operation with the South African border patrol. It's called Operation Hurricane. We, and the Zimbabwean police, have been tracking a network of smugglers for years. They export illegal animal products: ivory tusks, rare bird feathers, rhinoceros horn . . .

They smuggle the goods out of South Africa and Zimbabwe into countries where the regulations are more relaxed. From there, they fly or ship the contraband to the East Asian markets."

"This is why you're on the Safari Star?" asked Liana.

"Yes. We received word that one of the smugglers would be disguised as a passenger, taking a shipment into Zambia. Trains are searched less rigorously than planes and ships—especially luxury routes. Tomorrow, at Victoria Falls, Zambian officers are primed to carry out a sting operation when the smuggler delivers the goods to their contact. I'm on the train to represent the South African force and make sure nothing upsets the operation."

"Why disguise yourself as a retired police detective?" Winston asked. "It's not a very good cover."

"Ha! You're right!" Erik Lovejoy nodded. "I had planned on being Benjamin Berkenbosh, a trainspotter from Cape Town, but when I arrived at the station, I ran into your uncle. Nathaniel Bradshaw blew my cover before I'd even gotten on the train." He laughed. "Best I could come up with in the moment was that I'd just retired. I had to tell the woman in the ticket office that Benjamin Berkenbosh was my cousin, and he'd booked my ticket as a retirement gift."

"Does Luther know?" Liana asked.

"None of the staff know—everyone on the train is under suspicion."

"So when Mr. Crosby died . . . ," said Hal.

"It nearly ruined the whole operation." Erik nodded.

"Is that why you volunteered to lead the investigation into Mr. Crosby's death?" Hal asked.

"When Amelia Crosby cried murder, it risked the train being

impounded," Erik said. "That would have ruined years of police work. I was relieved we could prove it was an accident."

Hal's fear that they'd accepted the easy solution grew as he realized Erik's secret mission had made him keen to eliminate the possibility of murder. What if the detective was wrong?

Erik held up the piece of rhino horn. "Could you show me exactly where you found this?"

Hal nodded. "Uncle Nat said these carriages were once used on the Orient Express—that they might have had hidden compartments to help spies smuggle secrets."

"Have you found any others?" Erik asked.

Hal shook his head.

"Do you think the rhino horns are connected to Mr. Crosby's death?" asked Winston.

"I doubt it," Erik replied.

"What about that card Mr. Crosby sent Mama?" Winston asked. "He might have discovered the rhino horn and wanted to tell her about it."

"Mr. Crosby wasn't the type to care about animal rights." Erik looked skeptical. "And I still don't see how his death could be anything other than an accident."

"Do you know who it is?" Liana asked. "The smuggler, I mean?"

"I'm afraid not," Erik replied. "I had hoped someone might betray themselves on the journey, but Mr. Crosby's accident has made other detective work difficult."

There was a thud at the door, as if someone had fallen against it, and they all turned their heads, startled. Erik darted over, yanking it open, and jumped into the hallway. Right behind him, Hal heard running footsteps and the slam of the carriage door as someone leaped off the train into the darkness of the storm. Erik looked at him.

"Someone was listening to us."

CHAPTER TWENTY-FIVE

SNAKES ON A TRAIN

I love thunderstorms, and this one's spectacular," Uncle Nat said, as Hal flumped into the armchair opposite his uncle, suddenly feeling tired. "I saw Nicole safely back to her compartment. How was your mission?"

"I've got so much to tell you, I don't know where to start." Hal kicked off his shoes and sat cross-legged.

"I was going to get myself a hot chocolate before bed. Would you like one?"

Hal nodded, and Uncle Nat lifted the receiver of the telephone on the desk and placed the order. Then Hal launched into a description of his and Winston's descent into Mervyn Crosby's compartment, the discovery of the rhino horn, and Erik's admission to working undercover for Operation Hurricane. "But someone was listening at the door," Hal said finally. "Erik ran after them, but they'd disappeared by the time we got out into the corridor."

Khaya arrived with a silver tray carrying two enormous mugs of hot chocolate, with a cone of whipped cream on each, dusted with cocoa powder.

"I suppose the question is," Uncle Nat said, bringing the tray over, "was Mervyn Crosby's death anything to do with Operation Hurricane?"

"Erik doesn't think so," said Hal. "He thinks it was an unfortunate coincidence. But I don't know. I keep thinking about that card Mr. Crosby sent to Winston's mom. Was it to do with the rhino horn? Maybe he discovered it by accident and wanted to tell her?"

"I can't imagine Mervyn Crosby caring about smuggled rhino horn, unless he was the smuggler, which is unlikely, considering his wealth. He might have wanted to find out how much rhino horns were worth, I suppose."

"We only found a tiny part of a horn, which makes me think there was a whole one, and someone moved it."

"The smuggler would have been desperate to get it out of there before the police boarded at Musina."

"Which means it's still on the train, and so is the smuggler." Hal sipped his hot chocolate. It was sweet and comforting.

"But is the smuggler our murderer?"

"If Mervyn Crosby did find the rhino horn, they might be."

There was a growl of thunder, and Uncle Nat declared it was time for bed.

"Tomorrow's our last day on the Safari Star, and it promises to be a dramatic one. We set off for Victoria Falls after breakfast."

"Have you locked the door?" Hal asked as he climbed into bed.

"I did," said Uncle Nat in a reassuring voice, "and I'm right here if you need anything in the night." He turned the lamp off. "Sleep well."

***

"*HELP!*"

Hal sat up with a gasp. The compartment was dark.

"*HELP ME!*" a woman's voice screamed. It was Beryl.

"Uncle Nat!"

"I hear her." Uncle Nat was fumbling for his glasses. Hal turned on the light, and the two of them stumbled out of their compartment into the corridor. Uncle Nat rattled the handle of Beryl's door.

"It's locked," he hissed. "Beryl!" he shouted, hammering on the door. "Beryl, it's Nathaniel. Are you all right? Open the door!"

Beryl let out a terrified shriek.

Hal ran back into their compartment to the connecting door and flicked the hook up. He pulled at the door, expecting it to be locked on the other side, but it opened. Beryl hadn't locked it after their experiment with the fishing wire. He was about to step into the dark compartment when he felt Uncle Nat's hand on his shoulder.

"No. Wait here," he whispered.

Hal spotted Beryl on the floor in a shaft of moonlight, cowering at the foot of her bed in a long nightgown.

"Beryl?" Uncle Nat called out in a soft voice. "Are you okay? I'm walking toward you."

"*Stop!*" she cried. "Th-th-there!" She held out a shaking hand, pointing at a tangle of sheets on the floor. Hal saw a dark form, an intense shadow, moving through its folds. "*Sn-snake!*"

Uncle Nat froze.

"Help me!" Beryl squeaked. "Please!"

"I'll get Liana," Hal said, running before anyone could reply.

198

He bolted down the train to the service car, hammering on the door to Winston's compartment. Liana appeared, bleary-eyed.

"Help!" Hal gasped. "There's a snake on the train. Quick!"

Liana jumped into action, grabbing a pillow from her bunk and a metal stick with tongs at one end. "Go, go, go!" she said, and Hal sprinted back up the train with her racing behind him.

"Where is it?" asked Liana, as she came through the connecting door into Beryl's compartment. Uncle Nat was kneeling across from Beryl, the sheet with the snake in it on the floor between them. He was trying to keep her calm.

"Hal, can you find the light switch?"

Hal groped along the wall and flicked it on. Liana emptied her pillowcase, dropping the cushion onto the floor.

"We're all going to stay calm and keep very still," she said. "Mr. Snake here is very frightened."

"*He's* frightened!" Beryl gibbered. "What about me?"

"Where did it come from?" Winston asked, sleepy-eyed in the doorway. Chipo was in his arms.

No one answered. They were all holding their breath as Liana

approached the snake. "Who do we have here? Ah, a puff adder. Aren't you handsome? Hold still." She peeled back the folds of the sheet using the tongs, then pincered the snake, close to its head. It flicked its neck back, struggling, but there was nothing to bite. Liana held the pillowcase open and carefully lowered it in, tail first. Releasing the tongs, she clamped the fabric shut while she knotted it, carrying it at arm's length toward the bathroom, and putting it in the tub.

"Yuck!" Beryl struggled to her feet and scurried toward the door.

"Look out!" Winston cried as a bolt of black shot from the bedclothes toward Beryl's foot. A second snake was darting toward her ankle. It drew back its head, but before it could strike, Chipo leaped from Winston's arms, knocking the snake aside and rolling across the carpet with it in her claws. The snake hissed and spat at her. Chipo sank her teeth into the snake's neck. It struggled, then went limp. Chipo dropped it, dead, by the foot of the armchair.

Beryl looked like she was about to faint but was too frightened to let herself sink to the ground. She wobbled, and Uncle Nat leaped to her side, holding her up and letting her lean on him as he guided her out of her compartment and into his. "I nearly died," she was saying in a whisper. "I was nearly killed by a snake." She looked up at Uncle Nat. "Just like Cleopatra."

Liana picked up the dead snake with the tongs, depositing it in the bathtub, and began a systematic search of Beryl's compartment.

"Good girl, Chipo," Winston said, picking up the mongoose. "You're a hero."

"She was amazing," Hal agreed, his heart still pounding in his chest. He'd seen enough snakes on this trip to last him a lifetime.

"What's going on? Beryl?" Erik Lovejoy stood in the doorway, wearing a bathrobe and looking concerned.

Luther Ackerman, dressed in a colorful pair of striped pajamas and lace-up shoes, hurried up the corridor behind him. "Who screamed? Is everyone okay? I was in bed."

"A snake attacked me!" Beryl declared loudly through the connecting door. "Two snakes! They were in my bed. I could have died!"

"A puff adder and a boomslang," said Liana with a tiny nod. "Both are venomous, but thankfully no one was bitten."

"Oh, Chipo." Beryl held her arms out to cuddle the mongoose, but it ducked under Winston's armpit, hiding. "You saved my life." She turned to Uncle Nat. "And you were amazing. My hero." She grabbed his arm and hugged it, while giving Erik a pointed look as if he should have been the one to save her.

"Harrison, so cool in a crisis. You knew just what to do. And, Liana, thank you for coming to my rescue. My next book will be dedicated to you and Chipo."

Erik looked sheepish and went to see the snakes, offering to help Liana search the room again.

Beryl declared she couldn't possibly sleep in her compartment, and when Luther said that none of the vacant compartments had their beds made up, Uncle Nat suggested she sleep in Hal's bed. Beryl rewarded Erik with a sour look and immediately climbed into it, calling for chamomile tea and recounting her terror at finding snakes in her bed to Luther Ackerman.

Erik invited Uncle Nat to sleep in his compartment, and Liana suggested Hal could sleep top to tail in Winston's bunk, which he readily agreed to. The boys chased each other back down the train to bed.

"How do you think those snakes got in Beryl's room?" Hal whispered, sitting up in the bunk.

"Snakes live in underground burrows," Winston replied. "When it rains they come to the surface."

"Maybe they were looking for somewhere dry and slithered up into Beryl's bed?" Hal suggested.

"Two different venomous species of snake just happened to want to shelter in Beryl's bed?" Winston scoffed. "I don't think so. We're a foot off the ground."

"You're right," said Hal. "I think those snakes were put there on purpose. Someone was trying to kill Beryl."

"But who?" asked Winston. "And why?"

CHAPTER TWENTY-SIX

DIRTY LAUNDRY

Hal, wake up," Winston whispered. "They've found something!"

Hal felt Winston shaking him and opened his eyes. The compartment was lit with the blue light of early morning. "What's going on?"

"Last night, Mr. Ackerman asked Mama to search the train in case there were more snakes."

"Did she find any?" Hal drew his knees up to his chest and gave an involuntary shudder.

"I heard her talking outside in the corridor just now with Detective Lovejoy. She said she'd found something in the luggage car. I thought I should wake you."

"Do you think it's snakes?" Hal was apprehensive about facing more reptiles.

"I don't think so." Winston shook his head. "Let's go see."

"What about Chipo?" Hal looked at the mongoose, curled up on Winston's pillow.

"Let her sleep."

Hal grabbed his sketchbook from under his pillow and,

finding the corridor empty, the boys snuck barefoot through the service car and toward the sound of furtive voices. The door to the luggage store was open: a large cage where all the suitcases were stacked. Hal craned his neck to peer into the cage, and through the mesh he glimpsed Liana, with her hands on her hips, standing next to Erik. They were both looking down at something on the floor.

"The zip was open," Liana was saying. "I thought a snake could have got inside. I haven't looked in any of the others."

"Well, I guess we know who our smuggler is." Erik looked at her. "Will you stand guard while I go and wake Luther? He should know if I'm going to detain one of his passengers."

"Aren't you going to give him a chance to explain himself?"

"What is there to explain?" Erik sighed, looking back down and shaking his head. "But, no, you're right. I'll bring him here and show him the evidence."

"*Quick! He's coming!*" Winston hissed, pulling Hal backward, pushing him through a doorway and closing the door. The room was warm, and smelled of soap. They heard Lovejoy approach, pass, then walk away.

"Where are we?" Hal whispered.

"Laundry room." Winston opened the blind and let in a dim dawn glow.

"I didn't know they had laundries on old trains." Hal saw a double metal sink along the wall beneath the window. On a pulley above their heads was a clothes airer. Hanging from wooden slats were a pair of trousers, a leopard-print blouse, and some socks.

"Guests can have dirty clothes collected from the basket in

their room. There are no machines, though—they wash every-thing by hand." Winston perched on the edge of the sink. There was a high squeaking noise, and they felt the train roll forward, gently pulled by slow-chuffing pistons.

"We're moving," Hal said.

"What do you think's in that luggage cage?"

"Let's wait and find out." Hal stepped backward and tripped over a pair of boots thick with drying mud, almost knocking an iron off the shelf behind him.

"Shh." Winston giggled. "You want them to hear us?"

But Hal wasn't listening. He unwound the rope to lower the drying rack. As he'd fallen backward, he'd seen a flash of pink. "Winston, look—in the pocket of those trousers. Do you see?"

Winston gasped. "It's a pink scrap of cloth."

"Like the one we found in Crosby's wardrobe."

Winston pulled the ribbon of ripped fabric out from the pocket and handed it to Hal. "Whose trousers are these?" He held out the navy-blue chinos. "They belong to a tall man."

"That blouse belongs to Portia Ramaboa," Hal said. "She wore it the day before yesterday, at high tea."

"The trousers must be Patrice's," Winston said, his eyes growing wide. "But why would he have a torn piece of Mervyn Crosby's shirt in his pocket? Do you think there was a fight?"

Before Hal could answer, they heard footsteps. Winston drew the door back a fraction and both boys put their noses to the crack. They saw Erik, Luther Ackerman, and Ryo Sasaki enter the luggage store.

"Why is Mr. Sasaki with them?" Hal whispered as Winston opened the door wider. They crept out into the corridor.

"What is so important that you must wake me and bring me here?" Ryo asked Erik.

"Is this your suitcase?" Liana pointed down.

"Yes," Ryo replied, looking confused.

Hal went up on tiptoe so that he could see the case. It was red.

"Liana was searching the train last night after a snake was found in a guest's compartment," Erik explained.

"No one was hurt," he added, lifting a hand to cut off Ryo's worried look. "But when she was looking through this luggage store she found something else of grave concern." He looked at Liana. "Open the case."

Liana squatted down and flipped it open. Hal stood on tiptoe to see, steadying himself with a hand on Winston's shoulder. "Oh no!" he gasped.

"What is it? What do you see?" Winston whispered.

"A rhino horn!"

"I don't understand," said Ryo. "What *is* that?"

"It's a rhino horn," said Erik, "and I suspect you know all about them."

"Ryo Sasaki is the smuggler!" Winston was shocked.

"I know rhino horn was used in Chinese medicine a long time ago," said Ryo, "but this is an old-fashioned belief. The people who grind it to dust and drink it in water think it cures illnesses—but *I* don't. I'm a surgeon. I work in a hospital. I wouldn't have anything to do with that."

"Even if you don't believe in it," said Erik, looking down at the suitcase, "you know that a rhino horn is as valuable as a bar of gold."

"But that's not mine," said Ryo. "I've never seen it before!" He looked at Erik, dumbfounded. "Why are you doing this?"

"Because you're a smuggler, Mr. Sasaki," Erik replied. "If we were still in South Africa, I'd arrest you."

"I've telephoned the officials in Zambia," said Mr. Ackerman. "They'll be waiting for us when we arrive in a few hours." He shook his head. "I'm truly shocked, Mr. Sasaki."

"What? No! This is a mistake!"

"My only mistake, Mr. Sasaki, was trusting you," said Erik. "When we reach Zambia, you will be placed under arrest, not only for smuggling rhino horns but also on suspicion of murder." He gave Ryo an unflinching stare. "It seems I owe Amelia Crosby an apology. Her husband's death was no accident, was it?"

CHAPTER TWENTY-SEVEN

THE SASAKI SOLUTION

This is wrong," Hal whispered as the three men marched past. He looked at Winston. "We have to stop it."

"How?" Winston looked alarmed.

"We tell Uncle Nat." Hal opened the door cautiously. "He'll know what to do."

The boys crept down the train, their bare feet padding silently on the carpet as they followed the men. Erik took Ryo to the compartment they'd used yesterday for the interviews. Winston hung back while Hal crept into Erik's compartment and woke his uncle.

"Hal? What time is it? Is everything okay?"

"It's nearly seven. Quick, you've got to come. Ryo's been accused of being the rhino-horn smuggler," Hal whispered urgently. "And now Erik suspects him of murder!"

"What?" Uncle Nat reached for his glasses. "That's preposterous." He jumped out of bed. "Yesterday he didn't think the two things were linked. He was sure it was an accident." He pulled on his dressing gown. "What's made him change his mind?"

"I don't know," Hal said.

When they got to the interrogation compartment, Satsuki was standing in the doorway, confused and upset, talking to her husband in Japanese. His responses sounded calm and reassuring.

"Luther, take Mrs. Sasaki back to her compartment and get her a cup of tea," Erik commanded.

Mr. Ackerman nodded manically, guiding Satsuki away with his hand on her arm.

"Erik," Uncle Nat said, "what's going on? Is Ryo accused of something?"

"It's police business, Nat. Nothing to concern yourself with."

"Isn't he entitled to counsel?"

"He can call a lawyer when we get to Zambia," said Erik. "Please, I have this under control."

"If you're interviewing him now, perhaps I could stand in? If Ryo agrees?"

Ryo bowed gratefully. "Thank you." He looked at Erik. "I would like Nathaniel Bradshaw to be present."

"But he's not a lawyer," Erik objected.

"And you're out of your jurisdiction," Uncle Nat reminded him. "I think everyone would benefit from there being witnesses to this conversation. That way there can be a clear account for the officials in Zambia."

"Fine." Erik looked peeved.

"Hal, Winston, come in and sit on the sofa. You have your sketchbook, Hal? Good. You can take notes." He smiled at Erik. "Shall we begin?"

Erik looked as if he was going to protest, but instead he sighed and closed the door.

"Please could you explain why Ryo is being arrested?" Uncle Nat said, perching on the edge of an armchair.

"Mr. Sasaki has been caught illegally transporting rhino horn to a contact in Zambia. I believe he's part of a network of smugglers that I've been tracking for over a year. The horn in his suitcase is enough evidence to convict him."

"It's not mine," Ryo said firmly.

"Then why was it in your luggage?"

"It could have been planted there," Hal suggested.

"Hal, if you're going to be a witness, please don't interrupt," Erik snapped. "Mr. Sasaki was smuggling rhino horn, and I believe Mervyn Crosby discovered his plan."

"What evidence is there of this?" Ryo demanded.

"The note," Hal said under his breath.

"Yes, Hal, Liana's note," said Detective Lovejoy. "Mr. Crosby must have discovered Ryo was a smuggler. He found the horn and took it as proof, hiding it in his wardrobe. I imagine he planned to blackmail or exploit you. He confronted you out in Kruger Park, didn't he? Is that why Satsuki wanted to return to the train that afternoon? Was she upset?"

"She was tired," Ryo corrected him.

"You had to get that horn back and stop Mervyn Crosby from exposing you. Then, after high tea, you put on your surgical gloves and snuck into the Royal Suite, planning to remove the rhino horn. Hearing someone coming, you hid. Mr. Crosby entered, locked the door, and took down his hunting rifle. That's when you had the idea to kill him, wasn't it? You jumped out and grappled for the gun, shooting him. There were no fingerprints because you were wearing gloves. You posed the body and the gun to make it look like an accident. You took back the horn Crosby had taken from you, placing it in your doctor's bag—unaware that you'd left behind a small fragment that Hal and Winston found last night."

"But how did he get away?" asked Winston. "We would have seen him. The door was locked."

"Once you and Hal had gone into the observation car, Mr. Sasaki unlocked the door with Mr. Crosby's key," Erik replied. "He hoped to reach his own compartment, but heard Nat bringing Luther to the scene. He did what you had done—ducked into the open door of Patrice and Portia's room. He waited until Nat called for him, and appeared on the scene as if by magic, pretending to have heard the commotion, and came running with his medical bag."

"I did none of this!" Ryo said angrily.

"Being a surgeon, Mr. Sasaki knew I would ask him to attend to the crime scene," Erik went on. "He pulled out those same surgical gloves and joined Luther and me in the compartment. Once inside, he put Mr. Crosby's key back on the desk without us noticing, and set about persuading me that the most likely explanation was an accident, to stifle any further investigation."

Hal's mouth was hanging open. Detective Lovejoy's summary made sense.

"What you didn't know, Mr. Sasaki, was that Mr. Crosby had written Liana a note, asking her to meet him, perhaps so he could learn about the value of rhino horn, or to tell her about you. We'll never know."

Ryo looked stunned.

"But he has an alibi," Uncle Nat pointed out.

"From his wife," said Erik, his voice heavy with sarcasm. He shook his head. "I hope you realize she can be prosecuted if she lies under oath."

Hal felt a horrible twisting in his gut. Could Ryo Sasaki really be a smuggler and a killer? He listened as Ryo gave his own version of events: Satsuki had been with him at the time of the murder; he'd never seen the rhino horn before and had no explanation for how it'd gotten into his case. But there was nothing he could say to disprove Erik's theory.

"Yesterday you were convinced Mr. Crosby's death was an accident," Uncle Nat said.

"That was before Hal and Winston found the rhino horn in Crosby's room."

"Your evidence is circumstantial," Uncle Nat pointed out calmly. "There's no proof."

"We'll get it," said Erik. "When we reach Zambia, I'll have the train thoroughly searched. I've no doubt Mr. Sasaki is our man."

"Erik?" Ryo shook his head. "How can you think these things of me?"

"I'm a detective, Mr. Sasaki. I have to follow the evidence, even if I don't like it. And it all points to you." He sighed. "I was too quick to conclude that Mr. Crosby's death was an accident because of my role in the smuggling operation. I see that now."

"Well, then." Uncle Nat stood up. "Thank you for laying out your case so clearly, Erik. Come on, Ryo, let's get you back to your compartment. Satsuki will be worried."

"But . . ." Erik jumped to his feet.

Uncle Nat raised his hand, meeting Erik's glare with an icy one of his own. "I'm going to reunite Ryo with his pregnant wife so he can explain to her what's happening. I'm sure you wouldn't want to cause her any distress. The Sasakis will spend the rest of the journey in their compartment, until we are met by the authorities in Zambia."

Erik nodded.

"Hal. Winston." The two boys hurried to his side as Uncle Nat bowed to Erik and shut the door.

CHAPTER TWENTY-EIGHT

A PAPER TWIST

Shocked into silence by Erik's compelling theory about Ryo Sasaki, Hal and Winston followed him and Uncle Nat down the corridor. Winston was giving the surgeon's back an accusatory stare.

When they arrived at the Sasakis' compartment, Satsuki was alone. She stood as Ryo entered, pausing before running to embrace him, speaking rapid Japanese. Ryo replied in a soothing tone, but Hal could tell he was distressed.

"What can be done?" Ryo asked, closing the door and sitting in one of the armchairs.

"Erik's theory is persuasive, but the only evidence he has is that rhino horn," said Uncle Nat. "His case won't stand up in court."

"Can't you help?" Ryo looked at Hal. "You were part of the investigation."

"I'll try." Hal nodded. "Detective Lovejoy is jumping to conclusions. He doesn't have proof for half the things he said."

"But there is very little time," said Uncle Nat sorrowfully. "We'll be arriving in Zambia soon after breakfast. We should concentrate on finding you a good lawyer. I have a number of contacts who may be able to help."

Hal crossed the compartment to Satsuki. "Er . . ." He fumbled with his sketchbook and teased some pages from the binding. "Would you like to do origami? You said it makes you feel better."

Satsuki gave him a sad smile as she took the paper and sat down at the table. "You are kind, Hal."

Hal turned to see if Winston wanted to join them, but his friend was staring out of the window at the lemon-yellow horizon. All trace of last night's thunderstorm was gone.

Watching the way Satsuki folded and turned the paper, Hal tried to make origami of his own, but he got confused and gave up, turning it into a paper airplane and flying it at Winston's head.

"Hal? Winston?" said Uncle Nat. "I think it's time for breakfast. Let's give the Sasakis some privacy."

Hal nodded, realizing his feet were freezing and his tummy empty. He stood up.

"Here." Satsuki handed him a delicate, tightly folded swan. Hal carefully placed it in the folds of his sketchbook, thanked her, and followed Uncle Nat and Winston from the room.

"Shall I come and find you once I'm dressed?" Hal asked Winston.

"I need to feed and exercise Chipo."

"When we've finished eating, then. We can go over the evidence. Maybe there's something we've missed that will prove Ryo's innocent."

"I think he might be guilty," Winston said quietly, and bit his lip.

"What?" Hal was shocked.

"Mr. Sasaki seems like a nice man, but what do we really know about him?" Winston looked uncomfortable. "What if Detective Lovejoy is right?"

"But there's no evidence . . . ," protested Hal.

"It was fun playing at being a detective," Winston said. "But Erik Lovejoy is a real one, with forensic reports and undercover investigations. The rhino horn was *in* Ryo's suitcase . . ."

"It's okay," said Hal. He swallowed. "I'll find you later." And he returned with Uncle Nat to their compartment, a funny feeling in his chest.

"I hope Beryl's awake," said Uncle Nat as they approached their compartment door and knocked.

"Hell*ooo*?" Beryl called out provocatively.

"It's us, Beryl," said Uncle Nat. "We're here to dress for breakfast."

"Oh." She sounded disappointed. "Come in. Don't worry, I'm decent." Beryl was sitting up in bed. "I was hoping you'd be someone else. I *was* attacked by snakes, you know. *Two* snakes! You'd think that would earn me a morning visit."

"From who?"

"*Whom*, Harrison, a visit from *whom*." She flashed him a cheeky look. "And I think you know who. Last night at the Lodge, Erik brushed the back of my hand and told me I had pretty eyes." She fluttered her lashes.

"Erik's a little busy this morning," said Uncle Nat, walking to the wardrobe.

"Too busy for me, you mean?" Beryl pouted.

"He's accused Mr. Sasaki of being a rhino-horn smuggler," said Hal. "And of killing Mr. Crosby!"

"Does art mirror life, or life mirror art? That was one of the endings I was considering for my book. Either the kindly doctor or the quiet travel writer was going to be my killer."

Uncle Nat stiffened with surprise, and Hal tried not to laugh.

"Let me read you an extract." Beryl fished around in her handbag, then emptied it onto the bed. "Oh, blast! Where is it?"

"Am I going to be in your book?" asked Hal, gathering a clean set of clothes from the drawers.

"Of course!" Beryl said, getting up and looking about. "You die horribly. You realize who the murderer is just as you're set upon by a man-eating crocodile."

"Brilliant!" Hal laughed.

Beryl looked puzzled and went into her compartment, talking loudly so they could still hear her. "Everyone on board this train is a character in my book." There was a loud crash. "I've changed the names, of course, for legal reasons." Hal heard a series of thuds next door as he got dressed, but Beryl continued. "Truth is always juicier than fiction. For example, did you know Flo Ackerman hates her brother? Luther was the parents' favorite. He inherited the lion's share of the family business even though he doesn't know a thing about trains. Erik, of course, is my dashing detective—handsome and brooding. Did you know the darling man's brother died in prison?" Hal heard her opening and closing drawers. "He became a detective to try to solve the case that put him there. So tragic. And Amelia Crosby—she broke off an engagement with her childhood sweetheart to be with Mervyn! She's always regretted it."

Hal pocketed a bag of peanuts from the safari picnic that he'd saved for Chipo. He'd give them to Winston as a peace offering. He heard a tinkle that sounded like breaking glass, and looked at Uncle Nat as they both rushed to the connecting door.

"Beryl? Is everything all right?" Uncle Nat said.

"No, everything is *not* all right!" Beryl wailed. "I'm on the verge of a panic attack!" She stood in the middle of her compartment, the floor strewn with clothes and papers, bedding and emptied drawers.

"What's happened?" Hal asked.

"My journal is *gone*!" Beryl declared. "I keep it beside me at all times, but last night, because of those blasted snakes, I must have put it down, and I can't remember for the life of me where!"

"We'll help you look—won't we, Hal?"

"My *whole novel* is in there!" Beryl's voice wobbled. "But it's more than that." She shook her head to control her emotions. "It's . . . it's . . ."

Hal remembered how he'd felt when he thought he'd left his sketchbook behind in Kruger National Park. "It's like you don't know how to think without it," he said.

"Exactly." Beryl nodded. "That journal contains the workings of my mind, all my thoughts and observations."

"It's not just your book, then?" Uncle Nat said.

"No! It's everything. I write down what I see, hear, smell, taste, think. And, let me tell you, no one pays much attention to a batty woman scribbling in the corner—people reveal all kinds of good stuff." She covered her face with her hands. "Now the world will never know who committed *Murder on the Safari Star*."

"What did you say?" Hal asked.

"That was going to be the title of my book," said Beryl, wiping a tear from her eye. "What's the matter? Don't you like it?"

"Hal?" Uncle Nat frowned.

Hal didn't answer. A story was presenting itself as his drawings organized themselves into a flipbook in his head. It was an ugly story, and it frightened him. He forced a smile at his uncle and said, "It's the perfect title, Beryl."

CHAPTER TWENTY-NINE

TORN

A plate of scrambled eggs on toast sat in front of Hal, but he couldn't eat a mouthful. Dread gripped his stomach, and questions bombarded his brain. There was still a big blank in the middle of his picture. He needed evidence, but he was running out of time.

"What's wrong?" Uncle Nat asked, over a forkful of kipper. "Aren't you hungry?"

"Do you think . . . Beryl's journal could have been stolen?"

"Why would anyone do that?"

"They might do it if she'd spotted something important and written it down."

TING! TING! Luther Ackerman was standing at the head of the dining car, tapping a crystal glass with a spoon.

"Ladies and gentlemen, this is our last morning together on board the Safari Star. I am sorry our journey has been beset by such . . . erm . . . unpleasantness, but I am delighted to tell you that in twenty minutes we'll be approaching one of the most spectacular sights on planet Earth, Victoria Falls. I suggest getting to the observation car in good time to secure yourselves a prime seat.

Our staff will be joining us, too, to raise a glass and celebrate the end of this epic journey. The bridge over the waterfall is subject to a strict speed limit of five miles per hour, so there'll be plenty of time to drink in the view, as well as the champagne."

Hal wasn't listening to Mr. Ackerman. He was frantically flicking through the pages of his sketchbook.

"What are you looking for?" Uncle Nat asked.

"I drew a map of the train, marking where everyone was at the time Mr. Crosby was shot. But I can't find it. It was on a loose sheet of paper—it must have fallen out." Reaching the pages that held the two scraps of pink cloth from Mr. Crosby's shirt, Hal brushed one with his finger and glanced across the aisle to where Patrice and Portia were eating breakfast. "I need you to come with me," he said to Uncle Nat, getting up and stepping over to their table. "Excuse me? Mr. Mbatha?" The soap actor looked up at him. "I need to ask you something."

"Sure." Patrice flashed Hal a megawatt smile. "Is it about being on TV?"

"No," said Hal, sitting down at their table and lowering his voice. "It's about Mr. Crosby's shirts."

Portia dropped her cutlery with a clatter, and Patrice's smile froze.

"What do you know about that?" Patrice leaned forward.

"Everything," said Hal, placing the scrap of pink cloth onto the table as Uncle Nat came to stand beside him.

Portia put her hand to her head. "I thought you got rid of them."

"*I did*," Patrice said through clenched teeth.

"Would you care to explain?" Uncle Nat said, sitting down as Hal moved up.

"I had nothing to do with Mr. Crosby's death," Patrice said. "I swear it."

"But you *were* inside Mr. Crosby's compartment when he was killed. Weren't you?" Hal said, quietly.

Patrice paused, then nodded.

"You lost your temper when he insulted you at high tea," Hal prompted.

"I was enraged," said Patrice, his eyes flashing. "I couldn't let him talk to me like that. I had to defend my honor."

"You wanted to strike back?"

"Yes." His voice was a hoarse whisper. "I was so angry. I wanted to tear him to shreds. But I am not a violent man. I decided to tear up his pink shirts, to frighten him into being humble. I opened the connecting door between our compartments, using a credit card to lift the hook. I went to his wardrobe, pulled out the shirts, and ripped them into ribbons."

"But then Mr. Crosby returned," said Hal.

"I didn't know what to do! I heard him at the door. There was no time to run." He looked at Hal. "I grabbed up the shirts and hid in the bathroom."

"You were inside the bathroom while we were banging on the door, asking him not to shoot?" asked Hal.

"I heard you shouting, I heard him load the gun. I was frightened. He threw something soft at the door, then I heard him opening the window, then . . ." His voice petered out.

"I told him not to tell Detective Lovejoy," said Portia.

223

"You heard nothing else?" Hal was focused on Patrice.

"After the gunshot, I heard Mervyn Crosby fall to the floor. I opened the door a crack and saw him lying there." He shuddered. "I do not like blood, or guns."

"What did you do?" Uncle Nat asked softly.

"I had to get out of there quickly. I grabbed all the shirt pieces, ran back to my room, and dumped them in the laundry basket. I went to the compartment door, to see what was happening. I saw you and your friend walking away, but the mongoose spotted me and ran toward me. I threw myself onto my bed, pulled my mask and earplugs from under the pillow, and pretended to be sleeping."

"You're a good actor," said Hal. "I believed you were asleep. But how did you lock the connecting door behind you?"

"I pulled the hook down through the door using dental floss. A trick I learned as a kid. I'd set it up before I went in—I wanted the room to be locked on the inside so when Mr. Crosby found his shirts, he couldn't blame me." He shook his head. "After you boys had left my room, I panicked and pushed all the shirt scraps out the window."

"Not all of them," said Hal. "A scrap got caught in the wardrobe hinges when you pulled out the shirts, and this one ended up in the laundry room."

"I didn't kill Mervyn Crosby. You must believe me."

"I do," Hal said.

"You do?" Uncle Nat was surprised.

Hal nodded. "And now we have a witness who can testify that Ryo Sasaki wasn't in the compartment at the time of the murder."

"Ryo Sasaki?" Portia frowned.

"He's being investigated by Detective Lovejoy," Hal said, "but we think he's innocent."

"I don't want to be mixed up in a scandal," Patrice admitted, "but I wouldn't let an innocent man go to jail."

"Come, come, everyone!" Luther Ackerman strode up to their table, rubbing his hands. "Time to make your way to the observation car!"

Patrice looked nervously at Hal. "What are you going to do?"

"I won't tell anyone about the shirts, unless I have to," Hal replied. "But I have one last question." He looked at Portia. "On our first day aboard the train, I heard you two arguing. You told Patrice to act civil because there was 'more at stake' than his pride. What did you mean by that?"

"I didn't want his anger at Mr. Crosby to affect my relationship with Nicole," said Portia. "She wants passionately to make a success of her life, on her own terms, and I want to help her. She is a bright girl. She approached me privately and . . ."

"She has a lot of money to invest." Patrice finished off her sentence.

***

"I don't understand," said Uncle Nat as they headed toward the observation car. "Patrice was inside Mr. Crosby's room, but he *wasn't* the murderer. But there *is* a murderer?"

Hal sighed. "I think I know *who* did it. I just don't know *how* they did it." He tapped his forehead with his sketchbook. "I've a blank spot here." Satsuki's origami swan slid from the pages and fluttered to the floor. Hal bent down to pick it up. "That's where it got to!"

"What did?" Uncle Nat asked.

"Satsuki made the swan from my map—the diagram of the train, marking where everyone was at the time of the shooting. That's why I couldn't find it." He started to unfold the paper, and froze. He stared at it as he folded it back, then unfolded it again. Lines on the paper came together and apart. His mouth fell open. "I know what happened!" Hal looked at his uncle with wide eyes. "I know how Mr. Crosby was murdered. And if we don't prove it before we cross the waterfall, it'll be too late!"

CHAPTER THIRTY

VICTORIA FALLS

Hal spun round and bolted back through the empty dining car.

"Wait, Hal!" Uncle Nat hurried after him, limping. "Where are you going?"

"To the laundry room," Hal called over his shoulder as he ran out of the dining car and into the corridor of the service car beyond.

"Look out!" Winston cried as Hal barreled into him, and the two boys tumbled to the floor in a tangle. Chipo jumped from Winston's shoulder and glared at Hal.

"Are you all right? Is Chipo okay?" Uncle Nat helped both boys to their feet.

"What are you doing?" Winston said, rubbing his head. "Everyone's supposed to go to the observation car to look at the view."

"We have to get to the laundry," Hal said. "I've got a witness who proves Ryo couldn't have killed Mr. Crosby."

"He isn't the murderer?" Winston looked confused.

"No, and he isn't the rhino-horn smuggler, either. *Come on!*" Hal sped away.

227

Bursting into the laundry room, he looked about frantically. "They're gone!"

"What are you looking for?" asked Uncle Nat.

"There was a pair of muddy boots here this morning." Hal pulled out linen baskets and sent a stack of sheets flying as he searched. "Winston, do you remember?"

"Yes. They'll have been cleaned and taken back to their owner during breakfast."

"Oh no!" Hal turned to Uncle Nat. "That was our evidence!"

"For what?" Uncle Nat asked. "What's going on, Hal? What have you realized?"

Hal told them.

"*No!*" said Winston, in disbelief. "That's . . . No way!"

"My goodness, you're right," said Uncle Nat, the color draining from his face. "It all fits."

"And if we cross into Zambia . . ."

"It'll be too late," said Uncle Nat. He examined his watches. "But we'll reach the border in less than five minutes."

"We have to stop the train," said Hal. "We need more time to get the evidence."

"Stop the train?" Uncle Nat looked startled.

"We have one last chance," said Hal. "Winston, if Uncle Nat and I find a way to stop the train, can you get the proof I need? I think I know where you can find it."

Winston nodded eagerly, and Hal gave him instructions.

"Got it." Winston nodded and darted from the room, sprinting away down the corridor.

"We need to find the emergency brake," said Uncle Nat, glancing around the room. "There should be a button or a cord somewhere."

"Maybe out in the corridor?" Hal suggested.

"I don't see one," said Uncle Nat, following him out. "Let's try the kitchens!"

But the kitchens were empty, silent but for the clink of utensils swaying with the train.

"We'll have to stop the train ourselves," said Hal. "Come on!" They hurried back up the train toward the loco, passing the luggage cage and the crew's quarters. Uncle Nat heaved open the last connecting door, revealing the stubborn metal wall of Janice's tender and a drop down to the railway tracks. It was a dead end.

"We can't get through!" Uncle Nat shouted over the noise of the engine. "She's a Class 25NC, there's no corridor tender!"

"Can we can climb over?"

"It's too high! And much too dangerous!"

Through a gap in the trees, Hal saw the white mist rising from Victoria Falls. The track began to curve, and the train slowed down as they approached the bridge.

"Mr. Ackerman said the speed limit for the bridge is five miles an hour." Hal's heart was pounding in time with the wheels. "I think I could land the jump and run to the footplate."

"You are *not* jumping off this train." Uncle Nat pulled Hal away from the door. "You're staying here. I'll go."

The train's whistle blew, and the Safari Star emerged from the trees. The land on either side fell away as they rumbled onto the bridge, foaming water plunging into the deep canyon beneath them. White mist rose from the curtain of water and became clouds in the sky.

Uncle Nat stepped out of the door, grabbing hold of the ladder bolted to the service car. He paused for a moment and then jumped. Hal winced as his uncle landed awkwardly on his bad ankle and keeled over.

"*Uncle Nat!*"

Without giving himself time to think, Hal stepped out onto the ladder. He stared at the strip of tarmac sliding past the train, and, gritting his teeth, he jumped, slamming into the bridge with a *thud*, scraping his knee. He threw himself up onto his feet,

pushing forward as fast as he could, running alongside the train. The enormous locomotive was charging ahead, pouring black smoke into the sky. Hal sprinted as hard as he could. The hissing pistons and roaring waterfall deafened him. He advanced on the towering tender, his muscles burning, his lungs filling with smoke and steam.

"*Come on!*" He shouted at himself, willing his legs to run faster. Above him, the footplate grew closer and closer. "*Stop the train!*" he shouted. "*STOP THE TRAIN!*"

He could see the back of Flo's head in the cabin.

"STOP!" He waved his hands above his head as he ran. "*STOP!*" But no one could see or hear him. He grimaced, reaching for the ladder to the footplate. His outstretched fingers were inches away. With one last surge of energy, he lunged forward, grabbing the ladder and swinging himself up onto its rungs. He gasped, hugging it tight, before clambering up into the cabin.

"STOP THE TRAIN!"

"Harrison!" Flo jumped as he dragged himself onto the greasy cabin floor. Greg and Sheila spun round as he struggled to his feet.

"Stop the train!" he yelled. "It's an emergency!"

They looked at him with shocked expressions. No one moved. The far side of the bridge was getting closer and closer. Hal saw Sheila's hand gripping the red arm of the regulator, and he lunged forward, slamming down the lever of the brake. The wheels locked and screamed. The engine shuddered. Flo stumbled and caught the chain of the whistle, sounding high and bright over the roaring canyon as the train ground to a halt.

CHAPTER THIRTY-ONE

A POEM IN STEEL

Are you trying to get yourself *killed*?" Flo's face was red with fury. "What do you think you're doing?"

"I don't have time to explain," Hal said, dashing to the ladder. "The police will be here soon. Don't move the train until they say so."

"What?" Flo looked confounded by his behavior.

Shinning down the ladder, Hal found his legs were like jelly. For a moment all he could hear was the pounding of Victoria Falls. His T-shirt was soaked with mist and sweat. At the other end of the train, he saw people pouring off the observation-car veranda. Passengers and staff were spilling out, wondering why the train had stopped.

Uncle Nat was limping toward him, leaning on the railings to spare his ankle. "Hal! Are you all right?"

"I'm fine." Hal ran over to him. "Are you okay?"

"What's going on?" Luther Ackerman shouted as he marched toward the loco. "Flo? Why have we stopped?"

"Ask him." Flo pointed at Hal.

Hal looked past Mr. Ackerman to the passengers and crew, who were all walking toward him. When they were close enough to hear, he shouted: "*Listen!* Ryo Sasaki has been accused of smuggling and murder!"

Erik Lovejoy was standing beside Ryo, and put a hand on his shoulder to confirm this was true. A few gasps made clear not everyone knew what had been going on. But Hal had their attention now, and he needed to keep it.

"Ryo Sasaki is innocent!" Winston shouted, scrambling down from the service car. He ran toward Hal, clutching his rucksack.

"Did you find it?" Hal whispered.

"Yeah," replied Winston, his face lit up with excitement. "It was just where you said."

"Detective Lovejoy has built his case on firm evidence," Mr. Ackerman said, loud and clear so everyone could hear. "A rhino horn was found in Ryo Sasaki's luggage this morning." He gave Hal a pitying smile, and there was a wave of concerned muttering in response to this news. "I'm afraid we'd all rather trust a real police detective than a boy."

Hal glared at him. "The rhino horn was in Ryo's suitcase, Mr. Ackerman, because you put it there. *You* are the smuggler!"

"Nonsense!" Luther laughed, and a couple of passengers tittered.

"The Safari Star doesn't have enough passengers to fill her compartments, Mr. Ackerman. How do you make enough money to keep the railway running?"

Luther Ackerman stiffened. "We've been through some tough

times, but we're on the up-and-up now!" He punched the air.

Flo stepped down from the footplate, staring at her brother. "That's a lie." She folded her arms. "You've run the business into the ground."

"Is that why you're smuggling rhino horns and other illegal goods out of South Africa in secret compartments hidden throughout the train?" Hal pressed.

Flo looked at her brother with disgust. "Are you, Luther?"

"No! It's Mr. Sasaki." Luther pointed at him.

"This picture"—Hal opened his sketchbook to the drawing he had made at Pretoria Gardens—"is you being paid to take the shipment on board, isn't it? How does it work? Half up front and half on delivery?"

"Not this again." Mr. Ackerman laughed nervously, batting the picture away. "I've told you, I was buying steam-engine parts."

"Flo, is this Enzo?"

She shook her head. "Luther has nothing to do with the engines."

"You must have got a terrible shock when Mr. Crosby died, because you'd hidden rhino horn in his compartment."

"I didn't kill him!" Luther proclaimed, beads of sweat appearing on his forehead.

"You knew the police would search Mr. Crosby's compartment and that there'd be an investigation. After Mr. Crosby was found, you stayed in the compartment to make sure Ryo Sasaki and Detective Lovejoy didn't find the horns. Later, you let yourself back in using your keys and removed them, to hide elsewhere in the train. But you left a small piece behind—the piece that Winston and I found."

Winston nodded with pride.

"It was you listening at Detective Lovejoy's door when he told us about Operation Hurricane," Hal continued. "You learned the police would be waiting to catch the smuggler at the border, so when you thought everyone was sleeping, you planted a horn in Mr. Sasaki's luggage, planning to frame him. When Beryl was attacked by snakes, you seized the opportunity, asking Liana to search the train, knowing she'd find the horn and tell Detective Lovejoy."

Luther Ackerman started, as if he was about to run, but Flo blocked his path, and, quick as lightning, Erik was beside him, twisting his arm and pushing him down onto his knees. He pulled a pair of handcuffs from his pocket and snapped them on to Luther's wrists.

"So Mr. Crosby's death really *was* an accident?" asked Beryl.

"No. It was murder," said Hal, steeling himself for what he was about to say. "But it was made to look like an accident. When I started investigating, I got tangled up in how the killer could have got in and out of his room—but really, they didn't have to. Mervyn Crosby was killed from *outside* his compartment."

"By a trained assassin waiting in the bushes for the train to pass?" Beryl speculated.

"But he was shot with his own rifle," said Ryo. "The one he died holding."

"We *thought* he was killed by his own gun," said Hal, "because he was shot with a hunting rifle, and a hunting rifle was found in the room where he died. But we were forgetting—there are *two* hunting rifles on this train."

There was a murmur of alarm from the group.

"When the Safari Star traveled down the Dete straight, Uncle

Nat explained how rare it is for a track not to bend or curve. But the stretch of track around Rhino Rock is called the Hook, because it's a giant curve." Hal smiled at their confused faces. "A hunting rifle is designed to shoot over long distances. The Safari Star is nine carriages long. When the train turns a corner, it would be perfectly possible to aim a gun out of a window at one end of the train and shoot someone doing the same at the other."

"Well, I never . . . ," said Erik with a shake of his head.

"When Mr. Crosby died, he was leaning out his window, shooting at Rhino Rock. The killer was at the other end of the train, in Liana's compartment, and they shot Mervyn Crosby using Liana's gun."

"The note I received!" Liana exclaimed.

"Exactly," said Hal. "It wasn't a message from Mr. Crosby trying to confide in you—it was sent by the murderer, as a way to get you out of your compartment so that they could go in and shoot Mr. Crosby."

"But how could they have known when Merv would want to shoot a rhino?" Amelia asked.

"I was with Mervyn Crosby in the observation car when he thought he saw a rhino through his binoculars," Hal continued. "He said, 'Well, I'll be damned, it's the very place.' Someone had told him to look out for a rhino at the very point on the tracks where he would see Rhino Rock. They knew *exactly* when he would try to shoot at it."

"But wait," said Nicole, pushing her hair back over her forehead. "My dad . . . You all said you heard a gunshot from *inside* his compartment."

"Of course!" piped up Beryl. "He had his finger *quivering* on

237

the trigger of his hunting rifle. When he was shot from afar . . .
Bang! He jumps with the shock and fires the gun at nothing—
tumbling back through the window onto the floor."

"So there were *two* shots?" asked Nicole.

"Why, *yes!*" Beryl squealed. "I heard them!"

"You did." Hal nodded. "Beryl was the only person on board
to hear two shots. Her compartment is in the middle of the train,
and her window was open." He looked at Beryl. "You told us you
heard *gunfire*, and that you'd written the precise time down in
your journal. I thought you meant one shot, but you are always
precise with language—*gunfire* means *more* than one shot. I may
not have noticed—but the murderer did."

"So they tried to *dispatch* me, with snakes!" She gasped.

"The rain brought the snakes above ground. You keep your
window open because you hate air-conditioning. The murderer
went out into the storm, captured two snakes, and tossed them
into your compartment, getting their boots caked in mud."

"The fiend!" Beryl proclaimed.

"In the commotion caused by the snakes, the murderer took
your journal."

"Yes!" Beryl gasped. "It's missing!"

"There's only one person who was on the footplate when
Sheila told us about Rhino Rock," Hal said, "who was *also* present in Beryl's interview when she mentioned gunfire. Someone
who's a good shot and knows how to handle snakes." He turned.
"Mervyn Crosby was killed by Detective Erik Lovejoy."

CHAPTER THIRTY-TWO

NUTS AND BOLTS

Why would I kill Mervyn Crosby?" Erik said with a whisper of a smile. "I didn't even know him."

"You didn't know him," Hal replied, "but your big brother did, didn't he?"

"What do you know about my brother?" Erik stiffened.

"You told us Mervyn Crosby grew up in Johannesburg, like you. Then Nicole told me a story about her dad stealing a car when he was young and letting his friend take the fall. He let his friend go to prison for a crime he didn't commit. I think that friend was your brother. You told Beryl your brother was the reason you'd become a detective."

"He died in prison, didn't he, Erik?" asked Uncle Nat. "That's what you told me."

"Wait, what?" Nicole looked horrified. "Pop's Thanksgiving story was about your brother?"

"The car David was accused of stealing had been used in an armed robbery," said Erik. "He was charged as part of the gang."

"Oh . . . that poor boy." Amelia covered her mouth in shock.

"I spent fifteen years trying to get David acquitted, looking for proof that would link Crosby to the theft." Erik shook his head. "I failed. Mervyn Crosby got rich, and my brother became ill. It wasn't just a car he stole, it was my brother's life."

"You didn't know he was going to be on the Safari Star, did you?" Hal asked.

"When Mervyn Crosby arrived at the station, he didn't recognize me. He told me to carry his bags." Erik laughed bitterly. "It felt like fate was offering me a chance at revenge. He wanted to shoot a rhino. Liana had a hunting rifle. I knew about the Hook." He looked at Hal. "And there was a famous kid detective on the train whom I could coach into deducing what I wanted him to." He turned to Uncle Nat. "But I didn't decide to kill him until he kicked you. I told him he'd committed assault. Mervyn Crosby laughed in my face and told me that the law didn't apply to him, that he was above it. I'd only just buried my brother. It was too much."

"Oh, Erik!" There were tears on Beryl's cheeks. "You wanted me dead, too?"

"No, Beryl." His expression softened. "I put the snakes in your compartment to scare you away, so I could take your journal. You wouldn't have died. The Lodge would have had the antivenom."

"Oh, well, that's all right, then!" Beryl snapped sarcastically. "Lead a woman on and then drop venomous snakes in her bed." She leaned forward. "You heartless beast!"

Winston pulled the journal from his rucksack with a flourish. "It was in Mr. Lovejoy's compartment, just like Hal said it would be."

Beryl clapped with delight. No one spoke.

"Are you sorry Mervyn Crosby's dead?" Erik asked. "Any of you?" He looked at the silent passengers.

Amelia's mouth opened; she looked at Nicole, then closed it again.

"You were going to let me take the blame for Mr. Crosby's murder and the rhino smuggling," Ryo said angrily. "You treated me no better than he treated your brother."

"You are the same as Mr. Crosby," Satsuki said, looking furious.

"No," Erik replied firmly. "There wasn't enough evidence to convict you of murder. You'd never have gone to jail. Operation Hurricane is about more than one rhino horn. There's bundles of it stashed somewhere on that train." He sighed. "Harrison wouldn't drop the investigation. Even when I'd convinced him it was an accident, he kept working at it. I had to do something. I had to give him a plausible murderer. And when the rhino horn was found I thought you were working with the smugglers and saw an opportunity to pin the murder on you."

"You were afraid I would work out it was you?" Hal was surprised.

"A legitimate fear, it turns out." Erik smiled wryly.

"You'll give yourself up now, to the Zambian police, right?" Hal said.

"No. I don't think so." Erik pulled out his penknife, the blade glinting in the sun. "I'm not going to prison."

"Put the knife down, Erik," said Uncle Nat.

"I'm going to walk over to Zambia, where the police are expecting Detective Lovejoy, and tell them my version of events."

Erik backed away. "And while they're interviewing you, I'll disappear." He lifted the knife, a desperate look on his face. "Don't follow me. I'm better at throwing a knife than I am at shooting a gun, and I think you'd all agree, I'm a pretty good shot."

Everyone stood, frozen, watching him back away.

"Isn't anyone going to stop him?" Hal shouted. The grownups all looked at one another. "Somebody *do* something!" And he launched himself after Erik Lovejoy.

"Hal!" yelled Uncle Nat. "No!"

"*Nunu!*" Liana lurched forward as Winston dashed after him.

Lovejoy heard them coming. As he moved to throw his knife, Hal dived at the detective's legs, bringing him down with a clatter. The knife fell from his hand. Erik kicked at Hal, catching him on the side of his head with his heel, and Hal rolled away, clutching his face in pain.

"Winston!" Hal heard Liana's cry, and looked up to see Lovejoy standing with his arm round Winston's neck, pulling the boy backward down the track.

"Don't come any closer!" Erik shouted.

Liana, Uncle Nat, and Patrice, who were running, halted immediately.

"Let him go!" Liana bellowed.

"Winston and I are going to take a walk to the border." Erik was breathing hard. "I don't want to hurt him, but if you follow me any farther, he'll take a tumble off the bridge."

Hal saw terror in Winston's eyes. His stomach lurched as he glanced into the canyon. No one could survive that fall. Then he spotted a little nose, peeping out of the rucksack on Winston's back. He had an idea. Pulling himself up to his feet and ignoring his aching head, Hal said, in his most childish, scared voice, "Please don't hurt my friend." He reached his hand into his back pocket as he inched forward.

"He won't get hurt if you do as I say," Erik barked.

Winston was staring at Hal intently.

"Who's that?" Hal pointed his fist. "Is it a border officer?"

Erik turned to look and Hal threw a fistful of peanuts into the air over his head. Winston whistled and clicked his fingers. Chipo leaped up out of the rucksack and onto Erik Lovejoy's face.

"*What the . . . ?*" Lovejoy cried out, releasing Winston as he raised his hands to drag the mongoose off his face. Chipo panicked and scrabbled with her sharp claws, scratching his cheeks and neck. Winston sprinted away from the detective, into his mother's arms. Lovejoy swiped wildly at Chipo, and, temporarily blinded by the mongoose, stumbled against the railings, which juddered.

"Erik!" Uncle Nat shouted, limping forward, his face twisted in pain. "Watch out!"

Chipo jumped down, her back paws scratching his eyelids and drawing blood. Erik cried out as he fell backward, tumbling over the handrail.

Uncle Nat threw himself forward, his arms outstretched, seizing Lovejoy's calf as it flicked up. He roared with the effort and pain of stopping his fall. For one horrifying moment Erik dangled over the side of the bridge, the frothing canyon yawning beneath him like a giant's mouth waiting to swallow him whole.

Liana and Patrice were at Nat's side in a heartbeat, grabbing

Lovejoy's other foot, and together, hand over hand, the three of them pulled him back onto the bridge.

"Oh, Erik," Uncle Nat said with tears in his eyes. "Why did you do it?"

"He killed my brother, Nat." Erik trembled. "I had to."

CHAPTER THIRTY-THREE

THE NIGHT RAINBOW

The Bridge Cafe had a wooden floor, a straw roof, and was perched at the edge of the canyon. Hal was eating a pot of *nshima* and beef, looking out at the bridge over Victoria Falls. Murders weren't as fun to solve as he'd thought they would be. He felt confused about Erik Lovejoy. The man had saved him from a snake, and he'd liked him. But it was never right to take another person's life.

The passengers and staff of the Safari Star had been marched to the café by the Zambian police, who were interviewing them one by one. Sheila and Greg had driven the train into a siding so it could be searched, and afternoon had become evening.

Uncle Nat, Winston, and Liana sat on a long leather sofa opposite Beryl. Hal picked up his pot and went over.

"I hope they move us to the hotel soon," Beryl said as he sat down next to her. "I'm exhausted from all the drama and, frankly, I'm a bit whiffy." She sniffed her armpit and winced.

"What are you going to do with the rest of your trip?" Hal asked.

"There's an elephant sanctuary downriver that I thought I

might visit," Beryl replied. "Then I'm going back to England to write my book." Her eyes opened wide with excitement. "I've got a feeling it's going to be a smash hit. You must come and visit me sometime. We can discuss our favorite crimes."

Satsuki was sitting cross-legged on the floor with Nicole, passing time by showing her how to make origami birds from paper napkins. "If you come to Japan, Hal, we would be honored for you to be our guest," she said. "I am so grateful you solved this case."

"Your origami helped me work it out," said Hal, smiling back at her. "When you folded my map of the carriages, I realized that the two ends of the train could be opposite each other on a bend in the track."

"Harrison, I am indebted to you," said Ryo, coming over. "Should you come to Japan, to fill another sketchbook, you must visit us."

"I would love to," Hal said, beaming at Uncle Nat.

"I will show you the Shinto shrines," said Satsuki.

"And the superfast bullet trains?" asked Hal.

"The Shinkansen." Ryo laughed. "It is the least we can do."

Patrice returned from one of the vending machines that stood against the wall, a can of soda in his hand. He perched on the sofa beside Hal. "I wanted to say thank you," he said, his voice low. "For not mentioning the shirts."

"I should thank *you*," Hal replied. "I suspected Erik was the murderer, but I couldn't work out how he'd done it. As you were describing what happened in the compartment, I realized Mr. Crosby had to have been shot from outside."

"Well, I appreciate it." Patrice smiled. "Hey, Winston!" He

called to the opposite sofa. "I can give you that autograph now if you want?"

"Oh, er . . . thanks." Winston looked embarrassed.

"I'm sorry if Winston was bothering you, Mr. Mbatha," Liana said sternly. "He was told not to disturb the guests."

"Are you kidding? I love giving autographs. Hey, Winston, how would you and your meerkat like to come and visit the set of *Legacy*?"

Winston whooped, and Liana laughed. "He'd love to," she said. "But Chipo is not a meerkat. She's a yellow mongoose."

"Chipo is a hero," said Winston, stroking her. "She saved my life."

"I helped a bit," Hal protested.

"Maybe a little." Winston winked.

"When did you know Luther was the smuggler, Hal?" asked Uncle Nat.

"I was suspicious of him ever since I saw him taking that money." Hal sat back, realizing everyone was listening. "The night Beryl was attacked by the snakes, Mr. Ackerman came to her compartment wearing pajamas and lace-up shoes. That seemed odd. When the rhino horn was found in Ryo's case, I realized he must have planted it there in the night. When Beryl screamed for help, he threw on pajamas, arriving later than everyone else, pretending to have been in bed, but the shoes showed that was a lie. Then he made Liana search the train for snakes, knowing she'd find the rhino horn."

"Excellent deductions, Harrison," Beryl said, impressed.

"I wonder what will happen to Ackerman Rail now?" Uncle Nat shook his head. "All those beautiful trains."

"Now that Luther's disgraced, I expect the railway will be closed." Liana sighed. "I'll be out of a job."

"What about Flo?" Hal replied. "Can't she run the railway?"

"Her brother's crime will damage the company," Liana said. "I'm not sure passengers will want to travel on a train with such a tarnished reputation."

"Nonsense!" Beryl protested. "Everybody loves a good murder. It didn't do the Orient Express any harm."

"What if I buy it?" said Nicole. Everyone looked at her with surprise. "The Safari Star is a bit old-fashioned, but with a makeover it could be kind of cool. Beryl's right. Crime pays!"

Beryl beamed.

"Liana, you can run the safaris and look after the animals at the station," Nicole continued, getting excited. "Flo can run the train stuff, and Mom and I could do the rebrand and handle the marketing. With our media connections, it'd be huge."

"Have you ever run a business before?" Liana asked, frowning.

"You'd help me, wouldn't you, Ms. Ramaboa?" she called out to Portia, who was fanning herself in an armchair.

"I'd be delighted to help any business run by women," Portia replied. "I'm sure you will make it a great success, Nicole."

"Are you sure about this, Nic?" Amelia asked.

"I wanted to start a travel business with a

conservation focus." Nicole shrugged. "Why not this?"

"I think it's a great idea," Hal said.

"My goodness, everyone—*look!*" Beryl stood up. "I read about it in the guidebook, but I didn't think I'd get to see it."

"What is it?" asked Hal, as everyone moved onto the veranda.

"A famous spectacle," said Beryl. "Look—do you see?" She pointed into the night sky. Hal saw a cloud of white mist rising in the darkness and a beam of colors curving over the canyon.

"The night rainbow," Uncle Nat said in a hushed voice.

"When the night is clear and the moon is high, moonlight is refracted in the swirling spray of Victoria Falls, making lunar rainbows." Beryl fumbled for her journal. "I should write that down—it's rather good!" She scribbled furiously while the others watched the glowing colors shimmering in the night sky.

Hal crept away, unfolding his sketchbook and taking out his charcoal tin.

"What a lovely idea," said Uncle Nat, sitting down beside him and watching him draw. "You know, what you did today was very brave and grown-up. You should be proud of yourself."

"I didn't feel brave. I was scared. Erik tricked us all."

"But you outsmarted him." Uncle Nat nodded at the drawing. "Dark times can produce wonderful things." He sighed. "I really am very proud of you, Hal."

Hal looked out over Victoria Falls, watching the colors dancing in the mist, and smiled.

A NOTE FROM
THE AUTHORS

Dear Reader,

The railway journey in this book is a real one, although we have
not been fortunate enough to travel it ourselves. We have leaned
on research, and editorial advice from South Africa, to bring it
to life. As with all our books, we've taken liberties with the truth
where it helps the story.

The Real Safari Star

The Safari Star is fictional, but it's inspired by several famous
luxury railway journeys that you can take across South Africa.
The Blue Train, which travels overnight from Pretoria to Cape
Town, is the best known, but our journey's route is modeled on
one operated by a company called Rovos Rail.

The station at Pretoria Gardens is inspired by the real-life Capital
Park station in Pretoria, home to the headquarters of Rovos Rail.

Capital Park also has repair sheds, a railway museum, and some wild animals roaming the grounds, too.

The Real Janice

Many Class 25 locos were built in Glasgow and shipped to Africa for use on her railways. Class 25s had condensing boilers—which means they recycled their steam, turning it back into water in the tender once it had fired the pistons. This clever trick meant the steam locomotives didn't need to fill up with water so much, which was very important on the long, dry stretches of track. But condensing boilers proved difficult to maintain, and over time, most were converted back to normal boilers. Janice is a Class 25NC—the *NC* stands for "noncondensing," meaning her boiler was converted. As part of our research for this book, we went to visit the Buckinghamshire Railway Centre, which is home to the only Class 25NC loco in the United Kingdom. She pulled the famous Blue Train until the 1970s and was shipped back from Africa on a boat. Her name is Janice—that's where we got the name.

Rovos Rail operates a number of Class 25NC locomotives on their routes today. However, it's now uncommon for a steam engine to be able to make the entire journey from Pretoria to Victoria Falls, as water stops along the route are rare and costly to maintain. But we ignored this truth so that you could enjoy the magic of steam for the whole journey. We hope you don't mind.

The Railways of Southern Africa

In the late nineteenth century, the British Empire controlled about one-fifth of the world's population, with territory on every continent. It was said that the sun never set on the British Empire. At this time, a plan was devised to build a railway from Cairo to Cape Town—crossing the African continent from north to south exclusively through British-controlled land. Much track laid in Africa was part of this plan, but the route was never finished.

Many people argue that the British Empire built railways as a kind of gift to the territories it controlled. This is not accurate. The railways of Southern Africa were constructed to allow the British Empire to exploit the continent's natural resources—like diamonds, copper, and coal—more easily. This was often despite the objections of local people, whose opposition was violently quashed. Today, the railway's great feats of engineering remain, like the bridge over the Zambezi at Victoria Falls, but it is important we understand that they were not built for good-hearted reasons, and often at great human cost.

The Carriages

No carriages from the Orient Express were refurbished and used on trains in South Africa. This would have been impossible, as African railways use a different track gauge than European ones—the wheels would have been too wide apart to fit on the rails. However, the Orient Express really was used by diplomats carrying important documents across borders, and the train was notorious for use by spies and secret agents.

And Finally

None of the characters in this book are based on real people. Rhino Rock is an invention, and though there are many curves in the track, none is named the Hook.

If you're in the UK and would like to learn more about railways, we recommend taking a visit to the Buckinghamshire Railway Centre, or any of the other brilliant heritage steam railways and museums around the country. We also suggest a visit to the National Railway Museum in York, which is full of incredible locomotives and carriages from around the world. It's where Maya first fell in love with trains.

You can also visit our website to find great resources and learn more about Hal's adventures at adventuresontrains.com.

ACKNOWLEDGMENTS

M. G. Leonard

I'd like to use this space to thank our wonderful editor at Pan Macmillan, Lucy Pearse, who has helped us get the first three Adventures on Trains books on the tracks and brought the amazing Elisa Paganelli on board to do the illustrations. Sadly, this is the last book we'll work on together (as she's leaving to take a big fancy job at another publisher), but I feel lucky that I get to keep her as a friend, and, I hope, a reader. Thank you, Lucy. You are a legend.

Elisa Paganelli, with each new book you outdo the last. The illustrations and cover for this book are incredible. Thank you for all that you do, and for being the conduit for the way Hal sees the world.

Thanks to Jeri Wood, an adventuring spirit who told me all about her travels in South Africa and the night rainbow at Victoria Falls.

Huge gratitude and a loud *toot toot!* to every single person at Macmillan Kids who works on our books. You are an incredible team. Special heart hands go to Jo Hardacre, Alyx Price, Samantha

Smith, Sarah Hughes, and Ella Chapman. I can't wait to hug you all, once we're allowed to do things like that again.

Thanks to Foyinsi Adegbonmire, Emily Settle, Jean Feiwel, Liz Dresner, Angela Jun, Lelia Mander, and the rest of the U.S. Macmillan team.

Thanks to Kirsty McLachlan, my agent, who has set up Morgan Green Creatives in this tough year. You're an inspiration. The ride is always a joy with you.

The past year, 2020, has been a difficult year for me, and I'd like to thank Sam Sedgman for helping me to keep going. At times I didn't feel that I could. This writing partnership is more enjoyable and productive than I could have imagined when we first dreamed up the project, and I'm always learning from it. I'm constantly grateful to Sam for being who he is. Thank you, my friend.

I'm grateful to every bookseller, librarian, author, parent, child, and mongoose who loves and recommends our books. Thank you. Thank you. Thank you.

And thank you to my wonderful husband, Sam Sparling, and my sons, Arthur and Seb, who tiptoe around me when I'm bolted to my writing chair and celebrate every milestone, event, and achievement. I love you.

Sam Sedgman

This book—none of these books—would have been possible without our marvelous editor, Lucy Pearse. Sadly, this will be our last journey together as she steps down from the footplate to travel with another publisher. Thank you for being our guiding light through three brilliant adventures, and persuading us not to put a dead dog in *The Highland Falcon Thief*. I don't know what we were thinking! We will miss you terribly. Good luck on your travels—please send us a postcard.

Lucy comes from an excellent work family who have done so much to make us feel valued and supported. Samantha Smith, Jo Hardacre, Sarah Hughes, Ella Chapman, Alyx Price, and everyone else at Macmillan—thank you from the bottom of my heart for everything you've done to nurture these books and make them such a smashing success, especially in such turbulent times. You are all stars.

Elisa Paganelli continues to delight and amaze me with her incredible drawings of Hal and his adventures. She works so hard, so quickly, and with such exquisite skill, I can't believe we got so lucky to have her on board. The cover is a thing of beauty—I don't know how she does it.

Thank you to my brilliant colleague, confidante, and friend, M. G. Leonard, who has brought untold joy into my life through our writing partnership. Hard work has no right to be this much fun. Thank you for always reminding me of my strengths, and for persuading me not to complicate the plot so much. Here's to many more adventures together.

Constant thanks go to my agent, Kirsty McLachlan at Morgan Green Creatives, who would have no trouble running a railway. Speaking of railways, a special thanks must go to the Buckinghamshire Railway Centre, for letting us get up close and personal with Janice. Thanks also to the team at Macmillan South Africa for your advice. To my nephews, for the positive feedback. And to Sam Sparling, for all the lasagna.

Thanks as well to Foyinsi Adegbonmire, Emily Settle, Jean Feiwel, Liz Dresner, Angela Jun, Lelia Mander, and the rest of the U.S. Macmillan team.

To all the booksellers, librarians, and train enthusiasts who have pressed our books into readers' hands—a great big *toot toot* on the whistle! I feel incredibly lucky to have our books championed in so many quarters. Thanks also to all our readers, who have said such nice things. You're the reason we write.

I would be remiss not to thank Agatha Christie, who is ultimately to blame for all this. But also my wonderful parents, who introduced me to the world of crime by letting me stay up late and watch Poirot when I was probably much too young for it. They bought me murder mysteries by the bucketful, and indulged my need to make everything into a puzzle. Thank you for your unflagging support and tireless cheerleading. I love you.

And to Tom Leaper, my brilliant partner. When I have emptied my heart onto the page, he fills it up again with joy. Thank you for your kindness, your energy, and for listening to me complain about all my imaginary problems. I'm so glad we were lockdown buddies. I love you more than ever.